A Unico

The Meadows

By

Linda Menzies

This is a work of fiction and any resemblance to people, living or dead, is purely coincidental.

Chapter One *Secrets*

Every family has secrets. They lurk in cupboards, like spiders in dusty corners; they creak under piles of dead leaves in woods. There are illegitimate children who were adopted. The money stolen from frail old relatives. The clandestine affairs. Hastily arranged marriages and then early-arrived babies weighing eight pounds. The alcoholic uncles. The closeted gay aunties who lived with their best friend. Incest, abuse, cruelty, lies upon lies.   I'm not talking about these run-of-the-mill secrets, though. My secret is huge, unspeakable. I'll never be believed, so I've never shared it. I try to put it to the side, live my life as best I can. But now they are both clamouring for me to do something, to lay the injustices to rest at last, before I go. I've been on this earth before, and I remember.

I'm not talking Dr Who, HG Wells and the Time Machine, spiritualists with lengths of gauze or even about that spooky, scary feeling you get in an old house. Not talking about *déjá vu* either, or an over-working imagination .No, this is the full-blown, actually been here, remembering and knowing what really happened. Twice before, I have lived and died in Edinburgh and remember my life in both the 18th and 19th centuries. Both times I've died with the knowledge unshared. You could call this reincarnation, and maybe that's the nearest I get to explaining it, or giving it some sort of a label. I've always been Mary McGregor, I always look the same, but I have different families each time around. I now live in 2018, but I see the city's life and myself in previous eras, frequently, and usually at unexpected and often at awkward times. I have no control over these sightings and experiences, and no warning of when they will happen, or insight into the importance of these moments. Sometimes it feels as if I'm on a long piece of invisible elastic, and every so often I'm pinged back a hundred years or more. It doesn't make for an easy life, and the most frustrating part is that I can't tell what will happen in the future, or change the future. I only know what has been. Apart from the Edinburgh memories, sightings and returns, there is one more time and place I encounter, an earlier, shadowy memory of living in Dunfermline, working in the ancient palace as a kitchen maid. A memory arrives sometimes, usually when the moon is pale and high in the winter sky, and the winds scud clouds around. Then I see and feel the heat of a roaring fire, with sparks scurrying up the huge chimney. Dogs lie on rushes, gnawing at bones flung at them from the great table, and elaborate tapestries move slightly on the walls as the fierce winds hurl rain and sleet at the thick stone of the palace walls. I see myself washing platters, my bare feet cold on the flagstones and my hands red and chapped with the water. "Mary, lass, bring more rushes for the dogs, then tend the fire, it's dropping'", the housekeeper says. "And tie back yon hair, your bonny red curls are getting all tangled!" she said, without even turning to look at me. My hair was always wayward, and has been a trial to me over the course of several centuries.   Once, I saw the King himself, Robert the Bruce, a huge man who strode along the corridors, his followers hurrying to keep up with him. I was so awe-struck I couldn't speak, I just stood with my slopping pail of soap suds. He smiled down at me. "Careful, lass, you'll have that all o'er me!" I scuttled away along the uneven stone flags, leaving a trail of water behind me. But the Dunfermline memory is fleeting, and not troubling, so I must have lived and died a normal life then. How I came to be born in Edinburgh in the 18th century is not clear. I've done the research of course, with the aid of 21st century technology, but the tracing only gives me a little information, not much of it helpful. Likewise with my Victorian incarnation, there are gaps, unanswered questions, inconsistencies.

Edinburgh. This wonderful, vibrant city, where every stone and cobble, each close, park, building, has a story. Most days bring their own confusing experiences as I slip between times, like a car's gears sliding. I see, fleetingly, the Princes Street of the 1950s, with trams creaking along the middle of the road. The wide pavements are populated with ladies in fur coats, all wearing hats of course, with strings of pearls around their wrinkled necks, feet adorned with court shoes, making their majestic way into Jenner's tea rooms.

A blink and I'm back again to the present, to 2018, watching the new, smooth trams ding-donging their way along Princes Street, and children in pastel t-shirts and trainers jostle camera-clicking tourists on the pavements.

Supermarkets can be particularly problematic. One minute I'm at the deli counter in Sainsbury's, choosing cold meats and olives, when the scene suddenly changes and I'm staring at a grocer in a large white apron weighing ham from behind a scarred wooden counter. The fluorescent lights and whispering air conditioning above the cornucopia of delicacies disappear and instead I see open sacks of oatmeal, turnips and potatoes sitting on bare boards, the shop lit by gas lamps, puttering and flickering. Yesterday, the young man of the deli counter had to ask me three times if I wanted black or green olives.

Disconcerting, all this slipping around in time, living in 2018 but also still sliding about the last two centuries in Edinburgh, this teeming, creative city where I've lived three lives.

"Norman, that can't be the castle, surely," said a woman beside me at a bus stop in Princes Street. "It looks like a big house with an awkward terraced garden." Her Yorkshire accent cuts thickly into the keen city air, and I caught a hint of smoke about her. Her husband, immaculate in beige, turned to look more closely.

"Don't be silly, Ruby," he replied, with the weariness of habit. "Of course that's the castle. Look at the battlements, the flags flying."

Thing is though, that Ruby was half-right. When I ran these streets in the 18th century, the castle did seem more like someone's grand, big house, with a terraced garden that was indeed hard to keep because of the steep slope.

Sitting outside a restaurant in the High Street the other day, working on the Guardian crossword and watching the gulls cleaning up the human detritus, I suddenly glimpsed myself as I was in the 18th century, running barefoot along the cobbles, my red curly hair flying behind me, and snatching bread from the ground just as a surprised pigeon lunged for it. The muslin between times in this city is wafer thin some days, perceptible even to those without my peculiar and demanding history. Perhaps it is my familiarity with the place, but I sense the divide between past and present is so flimsy in this Jekyll and Hyde city, where six feet below my feet rats scurry amongst the honeycombed catacombs of the city, the seething black morass under the ancient cobbles.

At a nearby table, a young man, immaculately suited, smelling of Aramis, flips open his iPad, sips his coffee, crosses his legs. Beneath him, out of sight, Edinburgh's pipes and sewers gurgle and flow.

A divided city, where tramlines provide the physical embodiment. The trams, sleek, silent-running, with just a quiet 'ding' now and then, run on parallel lines, alongside buses and black taxis. The lines never meeting, never touching. The citizens too run on parallel lines, divided by money, opportunity, health and education.

The families who live in Stockbridge, Morningside, Trinity and the like are two children strong. These children, called Jocasta, Alice, Hilary, Hamish, Harry or Tom, go to private schools, by the skin of the family's financial teeth. Every set of cricket whites purchased, each school trip to the ski slopes means a tiny tightening of the belt, one less latte at Starbucks. No nasty-named Kylies, Waynes or Jay-dee Lees inhabit these stone-built villas or tasteful sandstone flats.

Here comes just such a family: George and Fiona and their children Saffron and Timothy, on their bicycles. They cycle everywhere possible, kitted out with fluorescent safety gear and annoyingly correct helmets, sitting proud in the middle of the lane, sure of their rightful place. Dad takes the bus to his office of civil service, or cycles in summer, his clips incongruous on his suit trouser cuffs. Secretly, he prefers pies to hummus and oatcakes, and buys a packet of B & H when he's away from home on courses. Fiona knows nothing of these small attempts at subversion. It's the best way to be, George accepts. He's been married a while…

The children have hobbies by the bucketful. They play sport – non-contact, of course – learn the violin, go to drama and art lessons, and at the weekend, they are taken to the Observatory, museums and the Filmhouse. They eat lots and lots of raw vegetables and fruit, and drink banana smoothies. The parents encourage Timothy and Saffron to save the whale, sponsor children's education in Africa and help poor broken-down donkeys. Fiona, who volunteers in a charity bookshop, does no paid work outside the home. "George earns enough to keep us, after all," she trills lightly, and thankfully turns back to making yoghurt, baking rustic loaves and knitting rainbow scarves for their lesbian friends, Pat and Jill. She helps George label and store their home-made wine and does a stint on the crafts stall at the local church – "although I'm not actually a believer", she confesses. Fiona can be found in certain haunts: little musty-smelling bookshops, John Lewis at sale time, Henderson's restaurant and in art galleries, sipping herbal tea in the cafe with like-minded friends.

"Terrible the way the school fees are rising," the women complain, biting into shortbread fingers. They regret falling or rising house prices, according to which side of the purchase fence they sit; make helpful suggestions on treatment for Sophie's chronic acne; and listen while Emily's mother blames the school, the exam system, the new syllabus and Emily's frequent headaches for her poor Highers results.

"She's so disappointed to have dropped to a C in Art!" complains Emily's mother. This last, the assembled women think, but do not say, is more due to Emily's known lack of intellect and her penchant for spending inordinate lengths of time shopping with her friends or going out drinking with her boyfriend Rod, who works for an insurance company and plays in a very loud heavy metal band at the weekends.

The marriages sometimes hit trouble, of course. George has a fling with his secretary and when he is found out, he and Fiona spend hours sitting across from each other at the pine scrubbed kitchen table, discussing, angsting, apologising and explaining (George), showing understanding tinged with anger (Fiona), until they reach a resolution.

George gives up the woman, who discreetly transfers to another office on a different floor, and replaces her as his PA with Mrs McGregor, a lady with well-cut grey hair, four grandchildren and an astonishing knowledge of filing systems, who is reaching retirement in two years, five months' time. Fiona, for her part, realises she will need to start having sex more regularly again with George, so it isn't confined to Christmas, birthdays and the occasional evening when she's had a glass of red wine too many and her very deep-rooted, rarely acknowledged and never discussed inhibitions are for once off-guard.

Fiona would much rather do anything than have sex, and has from time to time wondered if she might be a lesbian. However, she is realistic enough to figure out that she probably wouldn't want to sleep with a woman either. All that huffing and puffing and exchanging of bodily fluids, not to mention the rampant emotions unleashed. She'd rather have a cup of tea…

And the latte-drinking, Guardian-reading women like to think they sympathise with and understand their fellow women who live in in the city's housing schemes, who share the common spaces of the city, but often lead a different life.The women on the other side of the parallel tracks, who live in grey-harled council flats, give their children sausage rolls straight from Gregg's, because these are hot and tasty and filling. Their partners come and go, transient. There is love, but of a pragmatic nature. There are no late night discussions about the meaning of relationships, but instead, practical conversations about survival, children being fed, benefits or lack of them, work or lack of it.

And there are visits to young men in prison, who sit hunched across the table at visiting time, their right legs beating up and down under the table, white-faced, wanting home, wanting to begin again, but knowing that the same life awaits them outside.

Their stoical mothers or grandmothers have a quick cigarette outside the institution's gates before catching the series of buses back home. It's been a whole day's journey, to have just an hour, staring across a table and trying to find the right words to console, to sympathise, to express disappointment and anger and disillusionment. The right words never truly come forth, though, and nothing really changes. There is camaraderie amongst the women, a lending of money, and a sharing of food, cigarettes, take away meals and tins of cider. There is a basic acceptance too, non-judgemental, of the lifestyles of neighbours and family. The elderly and sick are looked after by extended families, who also accompany the ill to hospital and doctor's appointments. The old aren't left alone, but are visited by neighbours and family. There is friendship, a sense of community and a heavily-concealed tenderness of spirit.

Two sides, one city. In affluent Murrayfield, the blue, hazy smoke from barbeques pulls acrid scents of grilling meat into the lazy summer air, as men in weekend pastel polo shirts and big shorts cradle bottles of chilled beer and discuss the economy. Children with floppy blond curls and bags of confidence play quite roughly together on the manicured lawns while their slim and beautifully dressed mothers pick at salads and at each other.

Not two miles away, a man of Wester Hailes leans on his balcony, a roll-up and tin of beer in hand, contemplating the summer evening, watching his children playing in the dusty street, fourteen floors below.

Between these two homes, the zoo sounds echo oddly as twilight, then darkness arrives. The lion's fearful, exotic roar resonates in both communities, the rage of those trapped in high rise flats made noisy and articulate by the imprisoned beast. The lion, born in captivity and into Edinburgh chills and rain, seeks in his head for the ancient memory imprint of hot, dusty plains, freedom to lie by the water holes, to catch a stumbling deer. The zoo's monkeys chatter incessantly, their mocking sounds echoing across the stillness of the Sunday night city.

Because I have lived before, and remember, I know that even the poorest person lives in luxury compared with those around me in 18th century Edinburgh, where the rank closes teemed with dirt and germs; where even the best of parents struggled to feed their families and where shoes were only for Sundays...

***

I lived as Mary McGregor in 18th century Edinburgh's Old Town, and was familiar with the stews and middens, poverty and death. Friendships, love and affection sat alongside inequalities, disease and starvation.

David Hume lived down in the New Town but I saw him in the High Street near our close entrance a few times. My father was with me one of the times and told me who he was.

"Thon's a fine gentleman, Mary .He's got a great brain on him, they say, even though he doesn't believe in God," my father told me.

"Will he go to hell then, dad?" I asked, looking at Mr Hume.

"No, lass, I don't think so," my dad smiled. "God is forgiving to good people."

I saw Mr Hume another time, just near the Tolbooth, when I was running an errand for my mother and stared at him a little impolitely. He spoke to me.

"What ails you, lass?"

"My dad says you don't believe in God, sir, but you are too good a man to go to hell, is that right?"

David Hume laughed, but in a nice way, and gave me a farthing.

"Your dad is a clever man, lass!"

That Mary lives in me now, makes me smile, tweaks my memory, and gives me spirit and hope.

"Mary McGregor! Get in here this minute or I'll tan yer hide, lassie!" My mother, Isobel McGregor, called to me from the kitchen window, high above me on the fifth floor of our tenement, her face suffused with anger and her red hair wisping out from under the scarf she tied around her head each morning.

To point out that she couldn't tan my hide unless I went up to the house would just have got me into more trouble, so I held my peace for once and ran up the worn stone steps as fast as my bare feet would carry me.

"There you are: where have you been, lassie?" my mother asked as I came in the door, slightly out of breath. Ninety six steps to our flat.

I would later, much, much later, again live in a flat ninety six steps from the ground, not more than half a mile away from where Mary McGregor stood that day, ready for the telling off her mother was about to deliver.

"A've telt you till I'm sick, dinnae disappear like that, lassie! There's work to be done in this hoose every minute that God sends!" My mother always had a few chores for me to do each day. I ran errands, down to the grocer's shop for tallow candles, matches, and a twist of sugar or salt, a small sack of oatmeal or a turnip and a few carrots. I helped her clean the house, wiping down the old kitchen table with a damp rag or cleaning out the grate of the fire. I made beds and helped to look after my younger brothers and sisters.

Escaping when I could, I ran free through the stinking streets, past the one-legged beggar who stared at me, silent, with blank eyes, his ragged stump bound with torn strips of cloth.

"Dinnae be feart o' auld Jock," my mother told me one day when we passed him by on the way back home. "He lost his leg in an awfy accident, crushed by a cartwheel yin nicht. He'd had a drop too much ale and ran richt in front o' the horse. The puir beast shied up in terror and the driver couldnae pu' on the reins fast enough. Puir Jock didnae hae a chance. He tripped on the cobbles and the big wheels rolled richt o'er him. They say you could hear his screams a' the way doon tae the Palace!" she said, with a tiny hint of pleasure at the misfortune of another human being, meaning it bad luck wasn't sitting at her door, tempered by her own good nature and pity for Jock.

"Aye, he was a good worker, a cabinet maker, when he wasn't sitting supping ale," my mother elaborated. 'But the accident put paid to a' that," she concluded.
"Dinnae you go marrying a man that likes his drink too much, ma hen," she added, clearly thinking this was a good opportunity for some homely advice on the ways of the world.

I stood before my mother that day, under the dark, low ceiling of our main room, where we ate and chatted and argued, and often laughed. Mother and father slept in a curtained-off recess in the room, and the rest of us slept in the bedroom, the boys, Lachlan and Jamie in one bed top to toe and me and my sister Jean in the other. Baby Margaret slept in her cradle in the livingroom. Just as well we all got along, really, there wasn't a lot of privacy or space.

I escaped from the house whenever I could, running free and fast down the stinking High Street, dodging the sewage lying on the cobbles and always alert for the cry of 'gardy loo' which meant a householder above was about to tip a full chamberpot into the streets. I ran and ran, down past the foetid North Loch and down into the New Town to the cool elegance of the newly-built square–stoned houses and the clean cobbled streets.
Sometimes I was lucky and could slip into the private gardens unobserved, climbing quickly over the railings, and play hideaway amongst the trees, looking out for birds or little mice. I sat making daisy chains and watching the birds hauling worms out of the soft grass or carrying twigs to make their nests. Now and then, I fell into a doze and woke with a start to find out it was dusk.

"Run, lassie, run!" laughed men and women as I sped
through the darkening streets, rushing past the lamplighter
with his long pole, up through the stews and wynds of the
Old Town, my hair flying and my breath rasping. Sometimes,
I made it into the house without too many questions, but most
often I was in trouble for being out after dusk.

"Now Mary, I jist cannae hae ye awa' on yir ain when I dinnae
ken where ye are," my mother said, crossly, as I stood before
her that day, still slightly out of breath from running up the
stairs. "No' everyone is nice aroond here. There's bad folks
live in the cellar and caves over yonder…" She gestured
vaguely in the distance, but I knew she meant the rancid
underground cellars of the closes and chambers under the
bridges where the poorest people lived in the most utter
squalor.

I knew about the beggars, and not just the local ones like old
Jock with his stump of a leg. In my wanderings around, I'd
seen many beggars, dotting the streets like brown and grey
studs, or blown back into doorways, sitting cross-legged on
ragged mats. They had tin cups or battered old caps where
they collected farthings from people passing by. One day, on
my illicit journey down to the fresh, green gardens of the New
Town, I saw an old man with a little dog, sitting quietly on a
filthy blanket, his back resting against the railings of a private

garden. He wore layers of filthy clothes, rags really, and boots with burst toes. Around him on the blanket lay crusts of bread, a wizened half of a pie and a pile of small wedges of cake. Both the man and his dog sat with a terrible silence cloaking them, a stillness of utter despair. The poignancy of the broken up cake made me want to burst into tears, as I guessed instantly what had happened. Some rich lady had been walking with her children on the way to feed the ducks at the Water of Leith or a nearby pond and had given the old man the cake intended for the birds.

The old man sat, unmoving, although the dog looked up at my approach.

"Please, sir, here's an apple for you, and a wee biscuit for your dog," I said, reaching into my pinafore pocket and taking out my lunch.

He looked up at me, and I saw dignity and sorrow in his eyes. "Thank you, lassie," he said, taking my offering, studying my face.

"Ah once had a bonny wee lassie jist like you," he said, " but she's a' grown up and awa' a lang time ago, and Ah dinnae ken where she is."

I didn't know what to say to him, so I just smiled, patted the wee dog, and ran off to find a cool, quiet, green place to play, but I often thought about the old man and his dog and the daughter he had lost.

I was pulled from my reverie to my present situation as my mother continued to warn me of the perils of running around wild in the city. "You'll be the very death of me, Mary McGregor," she said, in an exasperated tone. "You should have been a boy and no mistake, all this running around and goodness knows what else. I dinnae ken whit tae dae wi' you. And that looks like another tear in your skirt, if Ah didnae ken better, Ah'd swear you'd been climbin' trees an' caught yir skirt on a branch!" Mother was right, that's exactly what had happened, but obviously I wasn't admitting to that. I shook back my hair but didn't say anything. Best not to begin a conversation on this subject as I knew how much there was to hide. Isobel McGregor pushed back her hair and looked at me again for a moment, and strangely, we had a rare moment of tacit understanding. My mother was a kind woman who loved her family and was always ready to help a neighbour in need, taking round a pan of broth if someone was poorly. Her fondly-remembered childhood on a farm in East Lothian contrasted starkly with her life in a tenement flat in Edinburgh's Old Town, and I suddenly realised how difficult it was for her looking after us all. I looked at her roughened, red hands which were rarely out of water as she washed clothes, pots and us children. It suddenly seemed so sad that this should be her life.

The understanding went both ways, though, and with an odd flash of insight I knew she had real fears for my safety but also loved my spirited nature. The moment ended with her folding me into her arms and giving me a hug, briefly kissing the top of my head. "Awa' noo and lift the bairn, it's time for her feed," she said, briskly moving me out of her arms and turning to stir the stew cooking in a huge iron pot hung on a hook over the fire. I expect it was the heat which made my mother have to wipe her eyes just then.

As I lifted my squalling baby sister Margaret from her crib, I thought, not for the first time, that as a family, we were lucky. My father, Davie McGregor, worked as a stone mason, a good trade and well paid, although it did mean he came home covered in a thick layer of dust every evening, which scattered across the newly-washed floors. We had a house to ourselves, with no lodger like most in our stair, and we were several floors up which meant we were free of flooding and had a bit of view across the city. The snag was that it was a long way down to the back yard where washing was pegged to hang limply in the dank, smoke filled air.

You shouldn't have favourites, whether things or people, that's the truth. Never have a favourite doll, or it will be broken, lost or stolen. Peggy, my little wooden dolly made from an old clothes peg and with an inked-in face, string hair and strips of rags for clothes, was lost somewhere on one of my runnings around. Safe deep in my skirt pocket one minute, she must have jolted and jumped out as I scampered up the High Street one day after a forbidden trip to Holyrood Park to see the wildlife which lived in and around the marshy bogs. I mourned the loss of Peggy, and even though mother gave me another peg to make a replacement, I never felt the same about the new doll. She was never my Peggy.

So, never have a favourite. Jamie was my favourite, without a doubt. That's why it was all so dreadful."Get away oot wi' you, and tak' yer brother an' a'!" My mother's exasperated tone was familiar. Too many people in too small a space; Jean and Lachlan fighting over a toy; the baby wailing in her crib and my father, unusually, home on a weekday with a bad cough.He was a big man and seemed to take up a huge amount of space in our livingroom. A rag to his mouth, he coughed and spat, rocking back and forth in his fireside chair. The smoke, the steam from the kettle and the odour from baby Margaret's napkin made the prospect of escape from the house a great prospect, even if I had to take Jamie with me.

Mother turned from the cooking pot hanging over the fire, her face flushed with steam, and a few wisps of hair straggling from her tied back bun.

"Be sure you're hame afore dinner time, Mary, and mak' sure he keeps his gloves on! "

I bundled Jamie into his thick jumper, hat and woollen mittens and, holding his hand, we went down the stairs, through the close and into the High Street.

"Now Jamie, you must dae what you're telt today, no running awa'," I told him, taking his hand. He was three, and inclined to dart away from me when we were out, especially if he saw something interesting – a rabbit, a nice looking stone, or a stick that he could use as a pretend sword. He looked up at me, his small white winter face spattered with freckles, his eyes blue and watery in the strong sunlight. As blue as the February sky, his eyes, light and clear.

"Aye Mary, but can we go to the ponds?" He looked up at me, his smile broad and dimples deepening. Even at three, he knew fine well I'd do what he wanted. Sometimes we went to the boggy marshlands in Holyrood Park, where he loved to see the frogs and tadpoles, and watch birds sitting in aloof serenity atop the dark, muddy waters, but today we headed in different direction. Jamie held my hand tightly, but his eyes wandered as he took in the sights and sounds of the bustling

High Street: gulls pecking for scraps of food, women with their skirts dragging in the dirt, and children playing with wooden hoops.

Tired from the longer walk, we were both ready to rest for a few minutes when we got to the green beauty of The Meadows and the Borough Loch.

"Here, tak' this, Jamie", I said, handing him a piece of bannock and a shaving of cheese. He ate quickly, talking as he stuffed the morsels into his mouth.

"Look, Mary, a big dug!" He shrank towards me. The dog was many yards away and on a rope held by its owner, but Jamie was frightened of dogs. As a toddler, he had been bitten on the hand by a neighbour's terrier. The bite wasn't serious, but he remained fearful of all dogs.

"Come on, we'll tak' a walk across the brig, Jamie", I said, taking his hand again. The walkways and drainage canals at the loch were being built and we pretended to walk the plank like pirates.

"I'm going to be the pirate king today," said Jamie, his face bright in the winter sunshine.

"Well, I just need to be the captured prisoner then, and have to walk the plank, eh?" He laughed. "I've got my sword, you need to dae whit 'Ah tell ye," he said, poking me quite roughly with the stick he'd picked up on the grass.

I pretended to be scared. "Oh, pirate king, be merciful!" I begged.

"Arrr," growled Jamie, poking me again.

It all happened with such speed.

The dog, which had been let loose to run, suddenly appeared right next to us, its rough coat bristling and tongue lolling out from its large mouth. Its breath rose like steam in the frosted air.

Jamie screamed and pulled from my hand, rushing along the pathway, the dog in pursuit of this new playfellow. The boy turned briefly, a white, terror-filled face with a silent black mouth, and the second scream didn't come. He was known to hold his breath to unconsciousness sometimes, in moments of fear or pain.

Time slowed and froze. My legs immobile, I saw Jamie's face turn blue, his eyes roll up into his head and with a ghastly grace, he toppled backwards into the icy waters.

The dog and I stood watching, for lengthy, endless seconds, as Jamie went under the water. The weeds at the water's edge hauled and trapped his thick jersey, his boots dragging him downwards.

The man, the dog's owner, ran past me and into the loch as my legs began to work again and I stumbled towards the water's edge, screaming and calling my brother's name over and over. The man too was impeded by the reeds and his heavy winter clothes, as he waded into the freezing water. The seconds turned to minutes as the man frantically scrabbled around to find the child.

Other passers-by had arrived by now.

A woman shouted: "'Am awa' for the polis" and ran off across the frosted grass, slipping now and then on the treacherous surface. A young man jumped into the water and ducked under the surface, his body rippling almost unseen beneath the blackness. His head broke through from the cold underwater, his face white and his chest heaving before he disappeared back down again.   It was the dog walker who took Jamie from the young man, whose third dive underwater freed the child from the reeds. In a grisly echo of a pass the parcel game, the blanched body of my wee brother was handed up from the loch into the arms of the older man.

Exhausted, freezing, dripping with slime and mud, the two men stripped off the boy's sopping clothes and pummelled his chest, breathing into his blue mouth. A woman wrapped her shawl around Jamie, weeping as she did so. A boy fished Jamie's cap out of the water, using the pirate king's sword. Jamie was carried by the dog walker all the way down to Infirmary Street, to the hospital. The man ran as fast as his soaking clothes and his dreadful burden allowed. One sodden mitten hung limply from Jamie's hand.

At the Infirmary, the doctor there listened for his heart but then just shook his head slowly and pulled the sheet over the child's lifeless face.

No-one reproached me. No-one punished me. I had my place at the graveside in the Canongate Kirk, with the rest of my family, wearing the same rough black arm band as my brothers and sisters.

My mother wore a black shawl, tied tight around her, with the baby bundled up inside, snug and oblivious. My father, trying to stifle his coughing as the minister spoke, looked as if his features had been carved in stone with one of his own chisels.

Jamie's small white coffin was lowered into the grave, next to his sister Lilian, the baby who had been born early, when I was four, and had only lived for two weeks. Too young to understand, I kept asking my mother why Lilian had gone to sleep and not woken up, and why did Jesus need to take my baby sister away to Heaven? Didn't he have enough people to keep him company there already that he needed her too?

At last, my mother had wiped her eyes and told me to wheest, sometimes babies were too little to stay in the world and had to be safe with Jesus and the angels.

"If you look oot the window and into the sky, Mary, you'll see wee white clouds, richt above the hoose. Do ye see them?"
I looked out and up. Sure enough, lots of wee white clouds in the blue sky.

"Is Lilian up there, on a wee white cloud? Which one is she on, mam?" I asked. "Why, the one richt above the hoose. Where else wid she be?" My mother held me close as she comforted me. After that, I waved to Lilian every day there was a wee white cloud above the house. Then Jamie came along when I was seven, and I sort of forgot about Lilian. Until today, till Jamie's funeral, when I remembered being here before. There were no reproaches, no punishments, and no recriminations towards me about what had happened.

The minister read from the Bible about Jesus and little children and spoke about people being taken before their time, then mother cried again and flung a single rose on top of the wee white coffin. Dad took a shovelful of earth and flung it into the grave, where the dry winter mud landing with a jarring thud on the wood. There was no retribution and no blame laid at my feet. Children died all the time in those days. They caught diphtheria and died a ghastly, choking death. They died of ear infections, cuts which festered, croup, measles and fevers. They died because, like my sister Lilian, they were born too early.

But this death was different. If I'd watched Jamie closer and held his hand tighter, or not taken him to the Borough Loch that day, he would still be here, with his cheeky wee freckled face grinning at me. The guilt went inside of me, coloured me, frightened and withered me. I wasn't consoled when mother told me Jamie and Lilian were both together now on the wee white cloud above the house. I just cried and cried. I stopped taking my younger brother and sister out to play. I only wanted to be near my mother and the baby, in the house, where I felt safe.

At school, I fell behind with my letters and numbers and I cried a lot at night, when the house was quiet and my sister was sleeping beside me. I looked out at the stars in the blackness and called Jamie's name softly, weeping, asking him to forgive me.

Chapter Two *The Letter*

I next lived in 19th century Edinburgh, where Victorian values were embedded into the stone villas of Morningside and society polarised into those who served and those who were served; into those who had full stomachs, nice clothes, education and those who scraped a living and who didn't know from one day to the next if there would be enough food for their families.

Where I lived was in a quiet, tree-lined street, in Morningside, with my parents and my very annoying older sister Elizabeth. My mother, Caroline, ran the house with the help of our cook/housekeeper, Mrs Ritchie and the maid of all work, Gladys, an unfortunate girl with a very thin, pink face, a slight squint and a nose which constantly had a dewdrop on the end of it.

"For goodness sake, lass, use your handkerchief!" I often heard Mrs Ritchie tell her.

My father, John McGregor was a partner in the Edinburgh law firm of McGregor, Pipsqueak and McTavish and spent his days doing very boring things to do with the selling and buying of property. One evening, when we were all sitting in the parlour, just before my bed time, I asked him if he enjoyed his work. He reflected for a moment and then he said, "Well, yes, I do, Mary. I like selling and buying houses and farms and fields for honest, decent people who have saved and worked hard to make a life for their families. "When I was a young lawyer, not long married to your mother, I did a different job, though. I had to go to the Sheriff Court a lot and speak up for people who had got into in trouble with the police."

He looked into the fire, where the orange flames were licking round the applewood logs which Bert the gardener had cut and stacked to dry out a year ago, when he had to fell the ancient tree.

Father gazed steadily at the burning, sweet- smelling logs and continued: "You see, Mary, sometimes people get into trouble just because they are poor. They steal food so their children won't go hungry. Or they rob a rich man of his pocket watch, to sell at the pawn shop.

"Sometimes I could help them, but often as not they were sent to prison, which is a terrible place to go. A black, dark, terrible place, Mary."
He looked across at me, the bleakness in his eyes painful to see.

"I've been lucky, Mary," he said, soberly. "My parents gave me and my brother and sister a good start in life. I never went hungry, we lived in a fine house and I went to a good school, and then off to the university to do my law degree. Your grandfather paid to get me articled to a good solicitor's practice down in the New Town. I worked hard, of course, but I had those chances early in my life.

"I look around me and I wish that everyone had those chances, not just people who are rich." I met his gaze. Sometimes my father was the only person in the whole household who treated me as if I had any sense or brains in my head. He talked to me almost as if I was a grown-up person. "So, father, Elizabeth and I are lucky because you make lots of money and we can live here, and we will get the things we want?" I asked, because I really wanted to know. He smiled at me. "Yes, my dear. I hope that Elizabeth, and then you, will marry well and give me some grandchildren to spoil. But I want you to learn things too, to work hard at your lessons here at home and when you are a little older, you will go to a school. Who knows? Maybe you will be a lawyer one day, and take over from me in the practice!"

He laughed heartily at his own joke. Of course I would never go to university, or be a lawyer. I was a girl.

I worked at my sampler, did a few simple chores around the

house and had lessons from a governess, Miss Sarah Hamilton, who came to the house daily and taught me reading, spelling, arithmetic, drawing and sewing. She sometimes took me for walks through the nearby parks, where we would sketch birds and flowers.

Miss Hamilton was ahead of her time, I now realise, as she sometimes took me for a walk through the Old Town. Father's carriage would drop us in the High Street, where he would also get out and walk the short distance to his office. "Now Mary, not everyone is as lucky a wee girl as you," said Miss Hamilton, holding my hand firmly as we picked our way along the slurry-strewn cobbles of Candlemakers Row down to the Grassmarket. "The children that live here don't have baths like you do in your house, and they don't get clean clothes very often, or even shoes to wear."

I thought that the children looked like they were having much more fun than I ever did, kicking an old, squashed leather ball around the street and playing with a puppy. They certainly wore very dirty, ragged clothes and Miss Hamilton was right, they had no shoes. I noticed that the girls had matted, sticky-looking hair and one of the wee boys wiped his running nose with the sleeve of his jumper. Mind you, so did Gladys our maid, if she thought no-one was watching her. I tended to notice these things, but would never tell on her to Mrs Ritchie or Mother. That would seem unfair, somehow.

However dirty they were, the children in the Grassmarket were laughing and running around, and it all looked very jolly. A couple of women stood at the entrance to their close, watching the children while they chatted. They wore old, rough-looking clothes too, but they did have shoes, and they laughed every so often. One woman had her hand on a battered old perambulator, which had a baby sitting up in it, watching the children playing. Suddenly, the baby began to cry and its mother swooped her arms down, in a swift, embracing movement and lifted her child close to her breast. "There, there, ma lovely bairn, ma best boy! Nae need tae greet, mammy's here for you!"

I don't know why I felt so moved to see that. The woman, the children, the baby were all ragged and dirty. I expect the daddies had to steal bread sometimes to feed them, and maybe end up in the Sheriff Court, and then into the awful dark horrible jail that Father had described to me. They didn't have nice things to wear like I did, and plenty to eat, and toys and books, but I realised they had things which I didn't.

I never got much fun at home, that was for sure. My sister Elizabeth was a lot older than me and had friends who came round for tea. Of course, I was never allowed to sit with them, which might have been interesting, I thought. Elizabeth even had a follower, Walter, who was an officer in the Royal Scots Guards, the cavalry regiment of the army.

Father knew Walter's family, so he was allowed to sit with Elizabeth in the parlour where they talked and read poetry. I know that's what they did, because I listened in at the door. I had to be alert though, because sometimes they rose suddenly and came to the door. Then I had to run and hide behind the hall screen, holding my breath and gripping my skirts so they wouldn't rustle and give me away.

I didn't know why Walter thought Elizabeth was so wonderful. She was always silly and giggly when he came round to visit, and when he had luncheon with us she behaved really oddly, passing him the water jug or the bread basket and just ignoring everyone else. I had to tap her on the arm once and say pointedly, "Please pass me the bread, Elizabeth, I'm still rather hungry!" She gave me a terrible look, just as well our mother didn't see it.

Walter was nice though, and sometimes he brought me a sugar mouse or a paper twist of barley sugar. One time, he brought me an old horse brass, which I polished until it gleamed. I put it on my dressing table alongside my collection of shells from the beach at North Berwick, where we went on holiday each summer to an hotel looking over the sea and out to the Bass Rock. I loved being at the hotel. The waiter always called me 'Miss Mary' which made me feel grown-up and important, especially when he pulled back my chair for me to allow me to sit down at the breakfast table.

Walter was always kind to me, he really was, despite me being Elizabeth's annoying little sister. That's why I feel so bad about what happened, about what I did. Walter knew how much I loved animals, and once, he took Elizabeth and me to see the regimental horses. We had to ride in a carriage away out of the city into the countryside, where the horses were out in the fields, or in their stables, their heads looking out over the half-gate. Elizabeth put her handkerchief to her nose as we walked through the stable yard, but I loved the smell and the noises the horses made as they whinnied and clattered round the yard with their big hooves clicking on the cobbles, their reins held tightly by the stable boys. I was allowed to stroke the nose of one big grey horse, and give him a lump of sugar. His nose felt soft, just like my toy velveteen rabbit at home, and his eyes were huge and brown.I loved it so much, I didn't want to come home again, but Elizabeth bundled me into the parked carriage with quite an unnecessary degree of roughness and ordered me to sit still and not move one single inch while she said goodbye to Walter. She took ages just to say goodbye to him, I was beginning to get very bored as there was nothing to do but sit.

Eventually, she climbed into the carriage beside me and the driver clicked the reins of his grey mare, as we set off back home again.

"Your face is very pink, Elizabeth," I said, as she settled her coat and skirts more comfortably on the narrow seat. "Do you think you might be getting a cold, or the quinsy?" When necessary, I could assume an air of total innocence, or concern, depending on which would either provoke Elizabeth, or keep me out of trouble, according to the circumstances.

Elizabeth flushed harder and made a show of looking in her handbag for a vanity mirror and her tortoiseshell comb. She combed her hair in a brisk and purposeful manner, tugging at her curls in a way which didn't look good for me. She glanced sideways at me for a second before resuming her perusal in the mirror.

"One day, Mary McGregor, you will go too far. One day, you will overstep the mark and then you'll know all about it!

She spoke with low, controlled anger and her voice was laced with venom and menace.

I said nothing, but sat back into my seat and pretended to be very interested in the fields and hedges we passed on the way back into Edinburgh.

Elizabeth was right, of course. One day I was going to go too far. And it was going to be my fault this time, not like High

Street Mary, who couldn't help what had happened to her brother Jamie.

When we got home, I ran straight to my room and began writing a story about Hector, the brave war horse, and his adventures in a place called Foreign Fields. My stories were all kept in a secret bundle underneath my winter vests and stockings. They mostly involved animals who could talk and who wore clothes, and had lots of adventures. Unlike my own boring life, where nothing exciting ever happened.

I'd overheard Mother and Elizabeth talking about Walter and his regiment soon going off to a place called Foreign Fields. It sounded quite a nice name for a town, perhaps it was like North Berwick, but far away over the sea, in Europe? I thought the horses would like being abroad in Europe. It sounded like there might be lots of warm sunshine there and fields where they could canter and enjoy the sweet meadow grass. I looked up my atlas and found the English Channel stretching between England and France. To get to Europe and the place called Foreign Fields, which I couldn't find on the map, Walter and the other soldiers would need to go in a ship, along with the horses. I hoped they wouldn't all feel seasick, that would be terrible, especially for the horses.

Mother had told me that when I was older and a young lady –
she did pause and look hard at me when she said 'young lady'
– but then continued, saying I would have the chance to go to
Europe. "Elizabeth will be going to Europe this summer, if all
is well and things are more settled with the troubles there,"
she said, as we sat in the parlour one afternoon sewing by the
fireside. I hated sewing with a vengeance, particularly
embroidery work, but it was quite nice sitting on a low stool
beside Mother. We'd just had some tea and scones, freshly
made by Mrs Ritchie not half an hour before. I usually had
milk to drink, but mother had allowed me to have some very
weak tea in a china cup, with a saucer, a rare treat.

"What will she do there, mother?" I asked. Mother paused in
her sewing for a moment and reflected. She smiled. "Well,
when I was Elizabeth's age, I went with your Aunts Jessie and
Bertha on a wonderful trip to Europe. Your grandmamma
thought we'd be safer altogether and would each enjoy the
company of her sisters. Grandpapa said it was all a terrible
expense and a waste of money, but we pleaded and cajoled,
and in the end, we got our way.

"Our old governess, Miss Amelia Mackie, came with us as a
chaperone. Oh, Mary, we did see some fantastic sights! We
visited Paris, with all its art galleries and museums, the stylish
gown and hat shops, and the jewellers. We took a boat trip on

the Seine, and were able to take our easels and paints down on the banks of the river, where we sat alongside proper artists painting the river and boats. Heavenly food, too, in the little restaurants: oh, how we loved the cakes!"

Mother was animated, remembering, and I suddenly saw the young girl in her face, as she must have been when she was Elizabeth's age. She looked into the fire and continued her story. "We went to Italy as well, to Florence, where we visited the Uffizi gallery, so full of beautiful paintings and statues, Mary! Then we went by train across country to Venice, where we went on a gondola punted by a man who sang to us.

"We had some time in Vienna, in Austria, where we learned new dances and ate all sorts of food we don't get at home. Finally, we reached Switzerland and had a few days high up in the mountains in a chalet, where the air was so fresh and crisp, and the snow glittering. The fire inside was so cosy after our walks outside. Oh, it was a wonderful trip!"

"What did you do when you came home again, mother?" I asked.

Mother's face briefly lost its glow and its animation. She looked a little sad for a few seconds, but then she smiled at me.

"Well, I came back home with my sisters, and we resumed our lives of helping grandmamma, painting, going for walks and doing charity work. That is, helping people who weren't as lucky as we were," she added, seeing puzzlement on my face. "We took old clothes, and medicines and sometimes food to people in our village who didn't have these things.

"Your Aunt Jessie was very keen on us helping other people in those days, and she used to argue with Grandpapa about why some people had to be so rich and some go hungry. I liked the sound of Aunt Jessie as a young woman, she sounded like she knew her own mind.

"Anyway," resumed Mother, "I had met your father a few months earlier. His parents knew grandmamma, and we were introduced at a dinner party he attended at our house. Not long afterwards, we began keeping company and he asked grandpapa if he could ask me to marry him. We became engaged and then married, when we moved into this house." She smiled. "When we had been married for three years, we were blessed with Elizabeth and then later, just when we thought we weren't meant to have any more babies, you came along."

Hmm. I don't know why anyone would have felt themselves blessed with such a silly and bad-tempered person as Elizabeth, but I kept my thoughts to myself, and quietly ate another scone while my mother was distracted by her memories.

"Have you been in my room again, and in among my things, Mary?"

Elizabeth was standing in the hall, her hands on her hips and a very cross look on her face.

If I had been innocent, I could, even at seven, have worked up a real head of indignation and injured innocence. Elizabeth would have apologised, and tried to make it up to me.

Perhaps she would have offered to read to me as a token of her remorse, although I was a perfectly competent reader, much better than anyone knew, even Miss Hamilton. I was keeping that bit of information to myself. It meant I could find out what was going on much more easily. People left letters and newspapers lying around thinking I wouldn't be able to read them. My mother once left a letter from my Aunt Bertha in Troon, lying on the dining room table after breakfast. I didn't quite understand it all, but it appeared that my aunt's parlour maid was getting married to the gardener's boy.

"All done in haste of course, the minister has been very accommodating in allowing such a quick ceremony," my aunt had written to my mother. "Of course, the girl has no parents living so I feel obliged to do what I can, although of course, Caroline, I'm bitterly disappointed in her. To think I harboured a girl with such loose morals!" I wondered what loose morals were, and what they had to do with harbours. Maybe the parlour maid had been out on a river trip with the gardener's boy and they hadn't tied the boat up properly afterwards at the jetty? Why they were getting married, and in haste, was a puzzle for another day.   I stared up at my angry sister with all the courage I could muster, but inside, I was churning with guilt and apprehension. She had caught me out.

I knew instantly that it had been the love letters. They were all tied up in a bundle with a pink silk ribbon. She kept them in her stockings drawer, along with the pressed flowers and the button off Walter's shirt.

Walter was clearly very smitten with my sister and poured his feelings into the letters he wrote to her. "Oh my darling, how I long to hold your pretty hand and look into those beautiful eyes of yours. Your cheeks are like rose petals and your smile like stars…" For a soldier, Walter was really very soppy, if you ask me. I don't know how he could bring himself to write such things! But if Walter was a big softie, my sister outpaced him by miles. Her journal, also kept in the stocking drawer, was a revelation. She recorded the events of every day in her life. Much of it made for extremely boring reading, involving detailed descriptions of visits to the hairdressers or the ladies clothing departments in Princes Street to choose new gloves, of Walter, how she felt as if she was swooning and feeling faint in his presence, longing for his next visit, worrying that he would be posted to some battlefront and hurt in combat. She describes him as her brave soldier, her cuddly wuddly bear and her soul mate. Goodness knows what her letters to Walter were like, if her journal was an example of how her mind worked. I just hope Walter hid the letters well from the other soldiers at the barracks, or he would be teased terribly, I knew. I'd been reading Elizabeth's letters, and her journals, for a long time of course, ever since I came upon them in one of my snooping forays. Well, if she wouldn't show or tell me things, I had to find it out for myself, didn't I? Unfortunately, on my last letter reading session in her room, I heard Miss Hamilton calling me as she walked along the hallway. I bundled back the letters hastily instead of putting them very carefully back in the order I'd read them. The most recent ones from Walter should have been on the top, and I'm sure they weren't…Elizabeth must have spotted the difference, and now she was extremely annoyed with me. Her pale face was set and hard, and her cheeks had two bright angry red spots on them. She was much taller than me, being a dozen years older, and I suddenly felt quite afraid that she was going to give me a severe smacking.

"I'm sorry, Elizabeth," I said meekly, my head lowered a little. Contrition seemed the best approach. "I just went into your drawer to get a handkerchief as I couldn't be bothered to go all the way upstairs to my own bedroom to fetch one." I made it sound as though we lived in a palace and my room was away along miles of corridors. In fact, although we lived in a good-sized villa in Morningside, my attic bedroom was only one short flight up from Elizabeth's rather grander bedroom.

Elizabeth was having none of it, though.

"You are a lazy and untruthful little girl," she said, almost hissing her anger. "You just like nosing around in my private possessions, which are nothing to do with you. I'm telling mother this time!" Whoops. That really was serious.I gulped, and tried quickly to bring on the tears by thinking about when our old dog Major had died at Christmastime, and how I gave him one last hug as he lay in his basket by the kitchen range, his eyes blind and his breath heaving. It worked, and I felt the big tears welling up in my eyes and rolling down my cheeks.

"I'm truly sorry, Elizabeth," I wept. "I'll do your chores for you for the next two weeks. For the next month. And I'll sort out the threads chest. Just please don't tell Mother, she will be so angry with me!"

I saw her waver for a second as she considered my offer, especially the bit about the embroidery threads. This horrible task, which came round once or twice a year, involved untangling scores of skeins of slippery coloured silk threads, or commonplace cottons, and darning wools, and winding them carefully and painstakingly onto bobbins, before returning them all to their correct drawers in the specially made sewing chest. It also meant pinning all the sewing needles in descending order or size, back into their cards. Mother became exasperated by the state of the chest, but could never discover the culprits who tangled up the threads in the first place, or stuck needles back randomly.

Truth to tell, all the women in the household who used the chest, except for my mother, were guilty of hastily sticking bobbins or reels back in, only too glad to have the task completed.

Elizabeth looked down on me again, and I knew it wasn't going to work. With a final furious glare at me, she stomped off towards the kitchen, where mother was talking to cook about the store cupboard supplies.

I went to upstairs and lay on my bed, awaiting retribution, my stomach fluttering.

It came soon enough, when our mother came up to my room later that morning.

She sat on the bed and looked at me.

"What am I going to do with you, Mary McGregor?"

She echoed the words of my 18th century mother but it wasn't really the time to try and explain that this wasn't a new criticism, and I'd been a trial to my mother a hundred years previously too. I had realised at a very young age that my other, earlier life had to stay a secret from everyone. Mother looked sad and disappointed as she looked at me from the foot of my bed.

"You know how upset Elizabeth is if she thinks you've been snooping and spying in her room and looking at her things. She is a young woman now, and deserves to have her privacy. You'll understand better when you are older, dear." I hoped her use of the word 'dear' meant I was off the hook, but it wasn't to be. My mother spelled out the punishment, sounding weary and annoyed at the same time. I was to do extra chores, including sorting out the sewing chest, for the next two weeks. I wasn't to have my friend Susan round to play for two weeks, and there were to be no puddings for me, for an entire week.

Susan I could take or leave, as it happened. She was an insipid girl, a year older than me, whose father was the minister of our church. Susan was a fearful child, terrified to do wrong, and always quoting bits of the Bible at me. I didn't mind going to Sunday School too much, as we got to make cards for Christmas and Easter and I quite enjoyed some of the stories the Sunday School teacher read us from a book called the Children's Bible, but I felt Susan's everyday heavy emphasis on religion, and the good behaviour which accompanied it, went too far. She didn't share my love of horses and she thought the stories I wrote and sometimes tried to read to her were very frightening.

All in all, we didn't have a lot in common. I did, however, enjoy visiting the manse because Susan had a very friendly, fluffy ginger cat with a new litter of kittens, which we were allowed to play with in the kitchen. Also, their cook made mouth-watering shortbread fingers and seed cake, and we were allowed to have these for afternoon tea when I visited. So, mother didn't realise that no Susan for a fortnight wasn't too upsetting for me, on the whole.

Being deprived of puddings for a week was another matter entirely, and one which cut me deeply. Like all seven year old children, I loved anything sweet, and our cook was famous for her jam roly poly and fruit dumpling puddings, all served bathed in a sea of delicious, creamy custard. Aggrieved, and angry at Elizabeth for inflicting this punishment on me, I sat on my bed after mother had gone. A couple of big fat tears rolled down my cheeks, not prompted by thoughts of Major this time. I buried my face in the pillow and sobbed.

A floor below, Elizabeth sat in her bedroom, at her dressing table and pulled out her hairpins. Picking up a silver-backed hair brush, a present from our grandmamma, she began to brush her long auburn hair viciously, each self-inflicted tug hurting her scalp. "I'll ask father to have a lock put on my bedroom door," she whispered to her reflection in the mirror. Her bedroom door was firmly closed, and the chances of anyone hearing her words were slim, but Elizabeth, with some justification, never felt truly safe from the prying eyes and ears of her dreadful younger sister. "She's just a spoiled brat!" she hissed to herself, noticing the red temper spots appearing on her pale cheeks. "Pampered and indulged, just because she's the baby of the family, and because she's so clever!" Elizabeth finished punishing her hair and sat looking at herself in the mirror. Two shiny tears ran slowly down her face. If only she had a sister nearer to her in age that she could confide in and go with to the stores in Princes Street, to choose winter boots or summer hats. If only Walter was in a position to ask her to marry him now, instead of when his career was more advanced. If only he didn't have to go off to this stupid war: where was the Crimea, anyway? "I expect Mary knows just where it is, and could point it out to me in her atlas, the little show-off!" Elizabeth muttered to her reflection. She sighed. If only she had the same intelligence and wit as Mary, then maybe father would talk to her more about the ways of the world, tell her more about his law practice, the history and the life of the city, and all the other many things he seemed so happy to chat about to her young sister. Then maybe she wouldn't feel so sad all the time, so lost and alone, Elizabeth thought. The only time she truly felt alive, she realised, was when she was with Walter, holding his hand, smiling into his eyes, and talking about the future they would have together. But when would that ever be? When could they be together, have their own home, and their own babies. Elizabeth continued to sit at her dressing table, her hair hanging loose and pretty around her milk-white, freckle-dusted face. Outside, the light began to fade as the Edinburgh winter sky darkened early. Sighing again, the sad young woman pinned her hair back into place and rose to light the lamp.

*****

Haunted was the only way to describe Elizabeth in the days and weeks that followed. Tormented by the what ifs, the whys, the sadness. My hated sister, confined to her room, weeping constantly, not eating and not speaking to anyway. Father and mother tried to help her, to comfort her, but she was beyond all consolation. Aunt Jessie came over one day and brought with her a potion she'd made up especially at her chemist's shop. "It might help her to sleep better, and the rest will mean she can cope better with everything during the day. Even if it helps her to get through funeral and the mourning period it will be better than nothing," I heard Aunt Jessie tell my mother. "Only time will really mend this, Caroline. You have to let her grieve and mourn for him in her own time. The poor, poor girl."

Worst of all, from my very selfish point of view, was that Elizabeth was being so nice to me. I went up to her room one day, and knocked timidly on the door. After a minute or two, I heard her voice calling faintly for me to come in. I pushed open the door and went over to her, where she lay on the bed in her dressing gown. The blinds were pulled down and the room was lit only by a lamp. Shadows played around the room in a sad and mournful way. Elizabeth's face was drained and grey, and she looked middle-aged, not a lovely young woman of 19.

I showed my sister the spring flowers I'd picked in the garden and placed them in a little vase for her. I put the vase carefully onto her dressing table, not spilling any water, and then sat next to her on the bed, slipping my hand into hers. She began crying again, in that quiet, terrible way that people do when their bodies are utterly exhausted with weeping and emotion. I began crying too and she hugged me close to her. I was crying for Walter's death in the Crimea, of course. It was so sad, and very frightening to me to think that someone I knew, who was so young, so handsome and full of life was now buried in the churchyard beside my friend Susan's house. But I was also weeping with guilt, shame and fear of discovery.

If only, if only. If only I could turn back the clock, wind back time the way father did when it was wintertime and he adjusted the hands of the old, chiming grandfather clock in the hall. If only I hadn't met Walter at the door that day when he arrived, out of breath, to see my sister.

Elizabeth was out with mother, visiting a poorly neighbour. In my view, the poorly neighbour would be all the worse for having the company of Elizabeth, but our mother thought otherwise. They set off together soon after luncheon was over. Miss Hamilton had left for the day and I was home with Mrs Ritchie and Gladys looking after me. Gladys opened the door to Walter's knock, and said Miss Elizabeth was out, but he could wait in the parlour with me.

He sat on the settee, and I took the low stool by the fire.

"I'm sorry, Mary," he said, after a few minutes, glancing at the clock on the mantelpiece. "I have to leave. My regiment is being shipped overseas to the Crimea tomorrow and I need to get back to barracks to organise our journey to the port. I can't wait any longer, I'm afraid."

He took out a letter from his tunic. "Would you please see that Elizabeth gets this letter as soon as she gets home?" He flushed and bit his lip. "You see, Mary, your sister and I had a little tiff last time we met… a misunderstanding…"

"What kind of misunderstanding, Walter?" I asked, innocently.

He looked at me, his large blue eyes wide and frank.

"Well, you might not know, Mary, but I love Elizabeth very much."

My expression was serene as I met his gaze. He didn't need to know about the letters, and me spying, did he?

"I'm expecting to be promoted soon, to a captain, and when that happens I'll be in a position to ask your father for Elizabeth's hand in marriage. She knows that I love her and want to marry her, but she thinks I'm dragging my feet over our engagement."

Walter ran his hand through his short, blond hair, looking miserable.

"And now, I've got to travel for weeks till we get to the Crimea, and fight in this war. I'm going away without saying goodbye to her, and making it all right again between us," he said.

Walter rose to his feet, straightening his tunic, and putting on his cap. "You give her that letter, Mary, and I'll bring you back a souvenir from the war. Maybe you'd like another horse brass, eh?" He smiled wanly, ruffled my hair, and left, his boots clicking on the wooden floor of the hall. I heard the gate creak open, and close, and watched him march along the street to where his horse was tied up.

Carefully, I slid the letter, sealed in its thick, creamy envelope, into my pinafore pocket. I had every intention of giving it to Elizabeth the minute she and mother came home. Over the years, I told myself this many times, but to little avail.

They arrived home soon, carrying a breath of the fresh winter air in with them. Mother went straight to the kitchen to see Mrs Ritchie about dinner, and I was left in the hall with Elizabeth.

She stamped a smudge of snow off her boots and unwrapped her long scarf, hanging it carefully on the hall stand alongside her tweed coat.

My hand was in my pinafore pocket, my fingers clasping the letter, when my sister started in on me. With hindsight, I knew that she wasn't really angry with me. She was angry with Walter's behaviour, and with her life and all its frustrations. But it was me who was standing there in front of her.

"What are you staring at, Mary?" she asked, an edge to her voice. She was fixing her hair, staring at her reflection in the long, gilt-edged hall mirror. She glanced over at me. "I'm still very, very angry with you for prying into my things. Mother was far too lenient with you. No puddings, indeed!" Her face coloured up with annoyance and frustration. The option was there for me, plainly. I could have just said nothing, and handed over the letter to her.

"You forgot to mention I can't see Susan either. And I have to do the sewing chest!" My indignation wasn't entirely genuine but I put on a good show of aggrieved innocence.

Elizabeth's pale complexion flushed high.
"You are an impertinent little madam," she said, in a low hiss.
"You have no notion as to how much I resent you snooping and spying on me, and looking at my private letters. I have no privacy in this house… if only…"

She tailed off, but I could read her mind easily. She wanted away, to be off with Walter, to be married, and to have her own house, her own servant, and perhaps children. She wanted to have control over her own life, and she certainly longed to be away from me. For the first time ever in our stormy relationship as sisters, I felt very hurt. I stood, silently, while Elizabeth darted another unfriendly look at me, and then flounced upstairs to her bedroom, closing the door with a firm click.

The letter lay in my pinafore pocket. My fingers smoothed the envelope. The parlour fire was low, but still emitting some warmth from its reddish coals. In seconds, the flames had consumed Walter's letter.

Gladys, quite naturally, mentioned Walter's visit that evening as she brought soup through to the dining room"Did you see Mr Kennedy, Miss Elizabeth?" she asked, ladling out father's portion from the tureen.

Elizabeth started. "Walter was here?"

"Why, yes, I let him into the parlour with Miss Mary, to wait for you." Gladys placed the bowl of asparagus soup at Father's place.

There was still a chance there for me to redeem the situation. I could have invented some story quickly, being much practiced at that, but once again, I took the other route. "Yes, he was here for a few minutes, Elizabeth. His regiment is going off to somewhere abroad." My air was casual. Elizabeth sat with her spoon poised in mid-air. "Well, what did he say? Did he leave a message, a note?"

Wicked. Yes, I was wicked, and stupid too. If things had turned out differently, it would all have come to light, the letter I didn't deliver, the conversation I had with Walter. But it didn't. "He just said he couldn't wait for you any longer and left." I replied, calmly breaking open my bread roll and began to butter it.

Father looked at me, hard.

"Are you quite certain that's all he said, Mary? Being a lawyer, my father knew when people were lying, but he wasn't able to fathom out the motive, so he was giving me the benefit of the doubt, I realised. Father was quite oblivious to the level of hostility which existed between me and my sister.

"That's all he said, that he couldn't wait for Elizabeth any longer and he was off. He seemed in a hurry to go and he seemed quite cross too."

If only I hadn't embellished that bit. The meaning was obvious to my sister, as I intended it to be: Walter was tired of waiting for her.

Wicked, I was downright wicked to let Elizabeth think Walter was cross with her.

Elizabeth turned pale under her freckles and carefully laid down her soup spoon on the placemat.

"I feel a little unwell, mother. May I be excused from dinner?" My mother and father exchanged a look. Mother said: "Of course, dear. Would you like Gladys to bring you a tray in your room?" Elizabeth shook her head, and walked slowly, with great deliberation, out of the room, closing the door carefully.

Chapter Three *1990s Unravelling*

I hate it, of course, I never wanted to have all of this knowledge. It has been hugely distressing to know what happened in the past and not be able to achieve justice. I feel as if I can't change anything, so my knowledge of the past does me no good. I can't predict the future either. It is also unspeakably painful to have had children and know they will not come back again, but I am condemned to keep coming back in a new body, to a new family.

Although… never say never…"Did you borrow my new cd?" he asked me one day. My teenage son, Steven, last in the nest, here with me in a tenement flat in the Old Town. It was a new nest actually, after what happened with his dad, all the trouble, the awful ending. Lucky I had Steven with me after what happened. Phoebe won't have anything to do with me. My dear, precious daughter, now a stranger to me, and it's my fault "No, of course not, I don't touch your music. It'll be in your room, Steven," I said, looking up from the book I was reading. "She's been playing tricks again. Expect I'll find it," he said, matter-of-factly. He turned at the door. "You do know that we have a ghost, don't you? An old woman with a long grey dress and a white apron. She's looking after us just now, I think, but I wish she wouldn't move my things around."

I sat, thinking for a bit, before I spoke. "Tell me a bit more about this ghost," I asked, making a major effort not to show my inner agitation. Perhaps Steven wasn't coping with the family break-up as well as I hoped and the ghosts were some manifestation of his traumas. Steven had already casually mentioned the coach and four he saw in the High Street one night, pounding over the glistening cobbles, then disappearing around Cockburn Street. And other stuff. He looked unperturbed. "Well, she's an old lady, with grey hair peeping underneath a funny sort of cap with a frilly fringe," he explained. A mob cap, worn by a Victorian servant, I knew immediately. After all, I'd seen plenty of them around me in the 19th century. "She was standing by my bed one night when I woke up, just standing there very still, looking down on me. As soon as I sat up in bed, she disappeared. I saw her another time, just standing still in the hall early one morning when I got up to go to the bathroom," Steven continued. "She just vanished again whenever I clocked her. Now, where is that cd? It isn't even mine, it belongs to Rory in my maths class, so I need to find it..."

He went off muttering. I didn't say anything at the time, but mulled it over. Could Steven possibly have seen Mrs Ritchie, the cook from Morningside Mary's household? I hadn't seen the ghost, so I couldn't be sure, but she sounded about the right age and description. There were so many things I knew, but still so many pieces of the jigsaw still to fill in…

"Does this scare you, seeing these things?" I asked Steven the next day over breakfast, when everything was very ordinary and normal. He chewed his toast while the clock ticked loudly and the radio mumbled in the background.

"Not really, it is just weird sometimes, seeing people or things who shouldn't really be there," he said. He was quite thoughtful for an 18 year old, really. "I sometimes wonder why I see these things and my mates don't. It means I have to watch what I say, or they'll think I'm nuts. Lucky we live in Edinburgh, eh? So many odds and sods wandering around in crazy costumes, especially at Festival time, I can pretend that's what I saw!"

He stopped chewing for a moment and looked at me. "But of course I know fine when I've seen a Fringe performer and when I've seen someone from the other side.

I looked at him again. "Some people just have extra sensitivity to atmosphere, and we live in a very ancient part of the city. Don't worry about this gift you have. It might come in handy one day."

I was matter of fact, practical about our lives, but the grinding guilt inside me never ceased. Especially hard was the loss of contact with my daughter who lived only a few miles away, but might just as well have been in Australia as far as I was concerned. Thinking of the loss of my marriage to Alan and the break-up of the family gave me that rusty blade in the throat feeling. I cried a lot, invariably in private I lost more than a husband, my home and part of my family, though. The break-up of the marriage decimated my social circle and showed me, with absolute clarity, those who were true friends, and those who were only there when everything was going well.

I had blotted my copy-book, set myself apart from the circle of married couples by leaving Alan, tearing up the family. I was a social pariah, and, worse still, a perceived threat to the other marriages. My best friend Marion, who stuck by me throughout, gave me the lowdown one evening, over a bottle or two of wine.

"Look, Mary," she began, "you're going to have to understand how it is, whether you like it or not and whether if seems fair to you or not. The women – our friends –all think that you are after their husbands now that you are on your own. I began to protest but she cut me off short, waving her wine glass around to emphasise her points.

"Yes, yes, you don't have to say anything, I know you aren't interested in anyone right now. In fact, Mary, I've always wondered a wee bit about you, maybe that you were drawn to other women…" she tailed off and waited for an answer.

I stayed silent. That was one place I simply wasn't going to visit right now, and certainly not with Marion at that moment. There was enough else going on that I wanted to discuss with her. That particular wooden chest of Sapphic thoughts had creaked half-open a few times during my marriage to Alan, but I'd slammed the lid down hard and pretended there was nothing to even think about, far less act upon. Although, deep down, I knew the chest contained the knowledge I suppressed, the feelings about the woman I'd seen in Tollcross weeks before my marriage. Would that ever happen, I wondered? I seem to have spent literally centuries waiting for resolution, happiness, or at the very least, peace of mind.

"I don't suppose you've got any fags, have you?" Marion was refilling her glass and topping up mine. I produced any emergency packet of B & H from the kitchen drawer, and we both lit up. The coughing of the unaccustomed smokers which we were subsided after a few minutes and through the wine sloshing around in my brain I made a mental note to open all the top windows before going to bed. Steven had watched his friend's grandfather die of lung cancer recently and was in a totally anti-smoking frame of mind. Marion, refuelled, now waxed lyrical about the mores of our social circle.

"Like I say, the women see you as a threat. The men see you as a helpless wee woman who won't be able to put up a shelf or change a plug, who needs them to coming charging along to the rescue."

She slugged back some wine and waved her cigarette around dangerously. "Moreover," she added, "you getting away like this, out from under the matrimonial shackles so to speak, is making the women a bit restless and the men a bit, well, jumpy. There's been quite a bit of angsting going on about the state of other marriages. You've acted as a... a catalyst, Mary!

She lit another cigarette and said, as an aside, "Have you noticed how much more articulate I get when I've had a few?"

I laughed heartily. It seemed such a witty thing to say. Marion was witty and clever with a degree in politics and philosophy; she was a talented photographer and exceptionally good at woodcarving; and she always looked as if she'd just stepped out of a beauty parlour. Unfortunately, she lived in the shadow of her husband, Tom, a successful businessman who had a paunch, a bald spot and an extremely high opinion of himself, without much justification.

Marion was much better company on her own, or at least, without him around picking faults and patronising her.

The evening gave me food for thought as well as a hangover, and her words explained why my invites to dinner parties had almost dried up, and why most of my women friends were suddenly too busy to come round for coffee. There were the practicalities too, which made life difficult at that time. Things taken for granted – a washing machine, dishwasher, freezer- all absent, at first regretted, but soon replaced by the quiet chores of soaking pots and rinsing glasses, as sun glazed the rims of plates, etching through the window panes. A primitive pleasure began to well up in me as sheets and shirts were sluiced in a bath-full of suds, then hug to drip, and ironed dry. Sometimes I longed for the garden and a bright, filled washing line of dancing clothes, but my garden memory had a shadow of anxiety cast across it, blotting the sun. At night, sometimes, there was the heavy falling into a sleep of exhaustion, in the still, warm room. Later, after several hours, there would be a lightening of sleep, almost waking, sensing the still unfamiliar surroundings. Remembering. Then, there was the drifting back into dream-laced sleep when the old fears would mingle with the new. There would be the grinding anxieties, the fear of the post arriving, the telephone ringing, the remembrance of the angry, sour man Alan had become, made worse by the hint of the strong and cheerful man he had once been. Just because of that school project, the revelations. Worries stacked up like a pile of pancakes in my head, slipping and sliding around, laced with the syrup of dread.

Dreaming, the shifting sands of memory parted and there were the houses, old and wretched down sinister, mossy paths, consumed with damp, populated by scurrying creatures. Or they were bleak, harled houses, surrounded by bitter earth, near to chip shops and cheap shops full of plastic goods and garish curtains. The dream moved on, through grimy flats, with strangers on the landing, to sadly perfect new boxes, with no room for books. Each had to be endured, made habitable and accepted as home. In the dream I have to do it all, panic in the night... Sliding back to morning and the welcome normality of sun-glazed windows, the city wakens to a glittering day. Down below, the Big Issue seller, strident and aggressive, begins the wearisome task of coaxing money from the flotsam and jetsam, from the brisk nurses slipping home off shift; the wandering, preoccupied students and the neat bank clerks, their spectacles glinting as they think pounds and pence. Down and out, the fat woman sits of the steps of the McEwan Hall, begging for cigarettes, money food. Incongruously, her hair is dye a startling, russet hue. Her slack jogging bottoms are dirty, smeared by the city. Slack-jawed, red-faced, the woman makes a dumb show of smoking, begging for cigarettes or money for tea. Sometimes others join her and they sit with cans of beer and watch life drift by. Curious, I wondered if they would move away on graduation days, when proud parents in new clothes watch their children, robed and hooded, move through to adulthood, away from them. The scene turns underwater green as they watch, then clears as they touch tissues to their eyes. At night, the fat woman goes into the haven of a night shelter, taking her off the sinister streets, and she sleeps the drugged sleep of the alcoholic, waking early, thinking of her first gulp of beer, frothing from the tin and sliding into her throat. I watched her, and remembered the drunken men sitting on the High Street when I lived there in the 18th century. They didn't start off that way, they all had a story, a sadness, and a misfortune. Our stair has twelve flats and inside each was a little family-two or three students together, a young couple, a single woman. They nod on the stairs, a faint hello or polite smile, but are unconnected. 'Only connect' said EM Forster. It is not yet time to connect again. This is limbo time, where I will consolidate.

I look out at the castle, illuminated each evening. Fierce, dominating, reassuring, it sits on the craggy rock, unchanging, a fixed point in a churning and tumbling existence. I think how my flat and the others in the area are built on the site of the ancient city wall. A good, solid place to be. My son sleeps soundly beneath his duvet from IKEA, posters on the wall, guitar propped in a corner. Lavender sachets beneath his pillows, and peace for us here, let him dream and relax.

Lavender does not work for me. I wake often in the night, and look at the castle, over the rooftops, and wonder, what next?

One night a faint sound jerked me from a dream of endless journeying on a bus which never reached its destination. It was no surprise to see, by the acid light of the moon, through pale curtains, a woman standing at the foot of the bed. Middle-aged, she wore the full, dark green dress of a Victorian matron, embellished with a gold locket at the neck. Her pale, smooth skin was unlined and her green eyes glittered and smiled at me. A shaft of moonlight stroked her tightly bound auburn hair, and there was a slight shimmer as she moved nearer.

At first she just looked at me. I was unafraid: of course I knew her, my aunt Jessie, sister of my mother and my aunt Bertha in Troon, when I was Mary of Morningside.

Jessie had never married, but had stayed with my grandparents into adulthood, and worked in a chemist's shop. Grandpapa hadn't been too happy at the idea of his daughter working, and grandmamma was very displeased. "Trade, my dear!" she said to my mother one day when we visited. "A daughter of mine, working! For a salary! If only that nice young doctor she liked hadn't gone off to Africa to be a missionary doctor, and died out there – so sad for his poor parents, and he an only son too!" Drawing in her breath, grandmamma had added: "And now she's going to live in Edinburgh, too, on her own!" I wanted to say that I lived in Edinburgh and liked it very much, but sometimes it was best to say nothing and just listen. Grandmamma was a raging snob – I realised that, even at the age of seven – but my Aunt Jessie had clearly been determined to do something useful with her life, and had trained as an apothecary, a dispensing chemist. The shop in Edinburgh where Aunt Jessie worked had drawn my interest, I remembered. It had elaborate lettering outside, and a swinging sign with a mortar and pestle. Mother and I had visited her a couple of times, coming all the way across town from Morningside in father's carriage. Once, Aunt Jessie took me into the back premises where coloured bottles lined shelves, and there were little baskets and boxes of dried plants and strange roots, which she used to make the herbal remedies and lotions. There were tubs of pills, and huge bottles of oils. My aunt told me that people brought back specimens from all over the world to make new concoctions and potions. It all looked very interesting, and I asked lots of questions. In the end, mother said: "Now Mary, your Aunt Jessie has quite enough to do without answering all your endless questions!"

A trip to a tearoom nearby made up for my disappointment in not being allowed to try out the mortar and pestle. So of course I knew who this night visitor was. I just hadn't expected her to turn up in the 21st century, at my bedside.

"I've come because you wanted me to," Aunt Jessie said at last, and her voice was so soft it was almost inaudible, it could have been simply the ivy leaves rustling outside the window. "You were always my favourite niece, you know. It was dreadful what happened to Walter, and to Elizabeth, because of it. All those deaths… all those families left bereft, because of that terrible war. Such a waste…" She stopped, caught up with her own thoughts, and looked at me again. "All is to follow, all this will be like a dream one day. You will step out of the shadows into the clear sunlight of a new day. You have the power to resolve this. You have more power than you can possibly imagine.

"It is not yet time to connect again, to change. But the time will come, and I will be there to help you."

I began to speak, but as I half-rose, she faded and disappeared, leaving only a faint trace of scent. In the morning, I found a twist of herbs lying in a muslin bag on the floor, with directions for use written in slanting copperplate handwriting, beautifully done, in sepia ink. 'Place in a warm bath and infuse aroma to ensure peaceful sleep,' said the label. I tried it and it worked. For the first time in months, I had a dreamless, peaceful sleep through to the 7am alarm clock wakening.

I made more of an effort after that, to be more cheerful and positive, but it was still so difficult. The injustice and the pain gnawed away at me. The pain I was causing, the pain in my heart every time I thought of Phoebe that last day, sat in me like some malevolent toad.

I slept fitfully, waking through the winter nights, hearing the winter rain and wind battering against the old casement windows. Aunt Jessie floated in and out of my dreams. Waking one morning after a particularly troubled night, where both Marys appeared vividly, and where I also dreamt, disturbingly, of Walter's lovely horse at the barracks, I found it hard to get going. I could scarcely concentrate at work.

The wise words of an old lady, a former neighbour, came into my mind one night as I lay waiting for sleep to arrive.

Effie was almost 90 when I first met her. She lived very near us in Edinburgh, in a small cottage at the end of our street. She was often in her garden, pruning roses or sitting on an old rattan chair at her front door, her head tilted and eyes closed against the sun. The old lady always passed the time of day with me as I struggled my way along the street with Steven in a buggy, Phoebe holding on to the pram handle, and our slow progress home made even longer by the weight of the shopping we carried. One day, we stopped to chat for a moment, and Effie invited me into her garden. It was a beautiful spring morning such as Scotland produces at times and reminds us all how lucky we are to live in this country. A blue and cloudless sky stretched above us, and there was the first hint of warmth in the air after a long, dreich winter. Phoebe found a twig and began digging up the earth in a border, while Steven slept in his buggy, a thin trail of dribble from his mouth heralding the start of another tooth emerging. I sighed inwardly at the thought of yet more broken nights, but enjoyed the few minutes of peace, just sitting on an old wooden bench near Effie.We talked of this and that, the garden, the weather, the children, the newly-formed Neighbourhood Watch committee. After a while, the

conversation drifted elsewhere, and I found myself telling
Effie how I found it quite difficult to feel settled anywhere. I
regretted the revelation almost immediately, as she quite
naturally began to question why I felt that way.

"Oh, we moved around a bit when I was a child, and I don't
ever feel anywhere will be permanent for me," I hedged. I
could hardly tell her of the innumerable places I'd lived over
the previous three centuries. Effie glanced at me, then, closing
her eyes tilted her pale, papery face towards the weak
sunshine. "I've had to live many places too, dear," she said.
"Some nice, and some not so nice. Some very bad indeed,
which is why I love my little house and garden here so much."
She looked at me again. "I always said that even if I had to
live in a barn, I'd make sure my corner of the barn would be
swept every day, and would have a cooking pot and a stove,
and would be as clean and homely as I could make it. For me,
and my children." I wanted to ask Effie more about her life
and what had happened to her in the past, but I didn't.
Instead, I reflected on what she had just said.

They were wise words, and they also applied very directly to
my present situation, up the 96 worn stone stairs to the attic
flat, where Steven and I lived in limbo. I had a gut feeling that
things were going to be alright, in the end, but we hadn't
reached the end. Not by a very long way.

Chapter Four *Seeking Resolution 2018*

I stood in Princes Street Gardens. An ice-cream vendor struggled to keep up with trade, children squabbled in the heat or tugged their parents towards the coolness of the fountain.

If only I could resolve it, sort it, and live out the rest of my life normally. See Phoebe. See my other grandchildren, yet to be born.

And of course, as well, there is the other person, who I kept missing, who was just out of reach, but who I knew was around somewhere, just waiting.

We slid past each other in Edinburgh so many times, missing one another. Each on the wrong side of the Canongate; ten minutes too late in the pub down the High Street; six rows apart in the cinema; a year apart at a party; miles adrift on new housing estates; days apart leaving the maternity hospital; a whisker apart in a record shop. We'd had all these times of just missing over centuries, apart from a glimpse one time, from my flat in Tollcross, when our connections were made and locked down .She was part of it all too, part of why I needed to make everything right.

Sometimes, when the moon was high and half- shrouded by scudding black-edged clouds I get a small, transient glimpse of the future, where I'm happy, with this person, and life is as it should be, perhaps as it is for many people. I don't know yet whether this will happen. I have many things to go through first. My courage falters, then I think of Phoebe, of Mary in the High Street, and of Mary in Morningside. Then I think of myself, today, of the injustice, the shadow over my life, a giant, and malevolent raven's wing blotting out the warmth of my sun or the silver stillness of my moon...

Chapter Five *The Death 1958*

"Mary! Hurry up or you'll be late for school!"

My mother tugged my unruly hair into pigtails, and tied them with green and white checked ribbons. I desperately wanted to have maroon or navy ribbons like the other girls, so that I wouldn't stand out and be noticed. Aged seven, a dozen years since the end of the war, I stood in my school blazer and hat, the school tie knotted firmly. I was about to set off across the city on the daily journey to my private girls school. This was one of the best schools in the city, where girls were encouraged to aim for anything they wanted out of life. Way ahead of its time, the future doctors, solicitors, teachers and businesswomen of Edinburgh sat in neat rows, ink wells filled, with serious work underway.

My little brain goes tick tick tick at school, as I learn and absorb new things each day. I am dressed for the part of serious schoolgirl, with a smooth cream tussore dress to wear in the summer, and a coarse-woven gym slip with a piece of ribbon with my house colour sewn across the top for winter wear.

My best friend Joyce lived in a bungalow near the Western General Hospital.

"Why do you live in a flat and not a house?" she asked me one day as we sat outside after our school dinner. We had been making the outline of houses out of fallen leaves in a corner of the playground and had had a disagreement as to the size of the sitting room. I wanted a small sitting room and a large kitchen. She felt the extra space should go to the bedrooms. While we argued, the chilly autumn wind got up and pulled the brittle beech leaves up into the air, quickly ending our game.

"My dad says you live in a council house. Why is that?" Joyce was carefully picking at a scab on her knee as she spoke. The subtleties of the Edinburgh class system were dawning upon us, slowly. "I don't know why," I said, truthfully. "I heard daddy tell mummy that when he gets to be a head of something they will have enough money to buy a house. He fills in forms all the time and always has lots of letters for mummy to post. And when he comes home from school he goes straight to his desk where all the letters have come for him. Do you think you have to be head of something to have a house that you buy?" Joyce shrugged and looked at me. "My dad works in granddad's garage selling cars. I heard him tell my mummy that if the old chap would just hand over the reins to him they could really clean up and we could move to a villa in Morningside, near where my aunt Ethel lives.

"I don't think they have a horse at the garage so I don't understand about that either. Unless it is in a field nearby and maybe dad has to clean up after the horse?"

"But why would having a horse make you able to have a house in Morningside?" I asked, genuinely puzzled. "In fact, if you had to feed the horse that would cost a lot of money so less for the house," I reasoned. "Marjory in the B class has a horse called Midnight who gets lots of sore tummies and she told me her daddy said a bad word when he opened a letter from the vet one morning at breakfast time."

Joyce looked at me. "All I know is that mummy says daddy needs to think about where he is going. I don't understand that either, because all he has to think about is getting in the car and driving to the garage and he knows the way after all this time.We looked at each other, uncomprehending in the ways of adults and money.

"Let's go inside and do our book now," I said, wanting to get the subject well away from where and how we lived, as well as wishing to return to the warmth of the classroom, out of the biting easterly wind. I got out the paper and pencil to continue writing about the exploits of Frisky the Fish. I wrote words in the bubbles which Joyce drew. She had the precious little cardboard packet of Lakeland coloured pencils, and claimed she needed them all for her drawing of the fish.

We worked happily together for a while, Joyce colouring in the detail of Frisky's scales and fins. She was very exact in her depiction of the fish, which resembled a rainbow-coloured, giant-sized goldfish. Each time she drew the fish, the colour sequence had to remain the same. For a child of seven, she had great tenacity.

It would stand her in good stead in years to come, when she was a partner in a prestigious Edinburgh law firm, dealing with business clients and handling eye-watering sums of money. She grew a deserved reputation as a stickler for accuracy and detail, greatly valued by her clients who knew that no unexpected problems would arise due to her oversight. I saw her mentioned in the business pages of the Scotsman from time to time over the years.

But then, we were just two small girls writing about Frisky the Fish.

Some years earlier, my mother, wearing her fur coat, took me across the city on a maroon bus to my entrance interview. My curly red hair was pulled tightly into ribbons and I was wearing my new bangle. In my handbag was a clean handkerchief. My new shoes pinched a little, but they were so delightfully shiny that it was worth the squeezed toes.

"Now, just tell me what you see in this picture," said the lady who had taken me through some elementary sums, reading and writing in the empty classroom.

The picture she showed me was of a woman in her kitchen, holding a biscuit-coloured mixing bowl and a wooden spoon. A child and a cat observe the process. I studied the picture for a short time from my position, seated on a small wooden chair. "Well, there's a lady baking a cake for tea and her wee girl is helping, and wants to lick the bowl afterwards," I said. "The cat is hoping that the wee girl will leave some for him to lick too, but he knows he can't jump on the table or he'll be in trouble, so he's sitting very still and quiet on the floor. The lady has pearls like my mummy wears sometimes when she and daddy go out, and she has on a pinny so she won't spill any flour down her dress.

"My grandma in Joppa has a pinny just like that, covered in flowers, and it ties at the back. It's very pretty, isn't it? The kitchen looks lovely and cosy because the lady has lit the fire, and is drying her tea towels on the fireguard. We have a guard to stop my little sister getting burned. She hasn't got the sense she was born with to stay away from the fire, my mummy says. It seems funny to be born with sense and then not have it by the time you are three, don't you think?"

I got a place at the school.

I liked it well enough except for the ribbon, and the duffle coat I had to wear, both not part of the uniform. Miss Sutherland, the primary school headmistress, was waiting in the cloakroom one afternoon, at the end of the school day. Holding the hem of my duffle coat with the tips of her tastefully manicured and beringed fingers, she looked down at me.

"Is this your coat?' she asked, disapproval edging her voice. I felt like saying: "Yes, Miss Sutherland. My name is on the coat peg," but that would have been construed, correctly, as impertinence, a heinous crime.

"Yes, Miss Sutherland," I said, lowering my gaze and feeling the hot, burning shame flushing up my pale, freckled face.

"Tell your mother that you require to wear a regulation navy blue knap coat as described in the uniform list which we supply to all parents", she said, icicles clinging to the words. I felt her gaze still upon me. "And ask her to provide you with maroon or navy hair ribbons, not any other colour." The silence around me in the cloakroom was palpable. My classmates, even at the age of eight, knew protocols had been breached and that I was in disgrace. I slunk out of the cloakroom, hot tears splashing down my cheeks as I walked towards the bus stop where I'd be taken to the other side of town, away from my classmates who headed for the villas of

Bruntsfield and Morningside, or the spacious sandstone tenements of Marchmont. Joyce, my loyal friend, walked with me in an uncomfortable silence, torn between her natural inclination to be on my side against the nasty Miss Sutherland, and her innate need for conformity.

We played our usual game of walking over the bottle green glass cellar grating outside a pub, and seeing our distorted legs look wavery and watery, but the tension was palpable. I kept having to reach into the pocket of my hated duffle coat to pull out my handkerchief and dab my eyes.

That day, as quite often, I saw one of the other Marys, Morningside Mary this time. She was in Charlotte Square, where I waited for my second bus home, my bus pass clutched in my hand. She was with her governess Sarah, and was so near I could have reached out my hand and touched her brown velvet coat sleeve.

I called out: "Mary, what do I have to do, why do I keep seeing you?" She stared straight at me for a second and it was strange to see myself so close up, and wearing those old-fashioned clothes. She opened her mouth to speak but then, as always, faded away.

Being Edinburgh, everyone in the queue looked straight ahead and ignored the small schoolgirl talking to herself. Joyce, who was still by my side, was unfazed. I often talked to myself as I worked out the complicated plot-lines for Frisky the Fish's latest adventures, and Joyce was accustomed to my inner dialogues sometimes spilling into spoken words.

***

Saturday at last. No school. The city's skyline was blurred with yellow fog from the chimneys of the factories. Overhanging the city too was the faint smell of yeast from the breweries. Our house was a new flat in a block of six, with balconies where washing grew and hung limp in the dank air. Every block belched smoke from the coal fires, and this mingled with the smell of fresh tar as pavements were laid in the new estate. A primitive, earthy smell mingled with the tar as workmen dug deep to lay the drains and pipes for the next blocks of flats. We were warned to stay away from the building sites, but of course we clambered around the building site at the weekends, dodging the watchman, and collected nails left lying, or pieces of green glass unearthed by the diggers. After George, who lived two blocks away from me, fell from a half-built wall and hit his head on some bricks lying around, all the children were told to stay clear of the building work and security was tightened on the site. We all watched, in silent horror, as George was carried by his dad across to the hospital, blood on his shirt, his face milk white, with his mother running behind, her coat flapping open, screaming.

"Ma bairn, ma bairn," she wailed, the words rushing behind her in the thick evening air, as she ran to keep up with her husband and his burden. George's head lolled back in his father's arms, his legs dangling like those of a grotesque, gangly puppet.

Fortunately, George recovered from his injuries, and was then envied for his prolonged convalescence at home, and absence of schoolwork, while his cracked skull healed. He wore a huge crepe bandage round his head, like a bizarre crown, and lay in comfort along the sofa, listening to the radio. While he recovered, we neighbourhood children visited him, bringing comics and sickly sweet smelling pink bubble gum. George's enforced inactivity allowed him to perfect the art of blowing huge bubbles with the gum, and he was thereafter known as Gummy George.

As a result of his accident, though, all the children were discouraged from any dangerous activities, which included not only staying well away from the building site, but also from climbing of any kind.

I was lying on top of the bucket sheds – strictly out of bounds as it involved shinning up a drain pipe and clambering onto the roof – with my friend Morag. The back green contained this brick built, harled outhouse with a flat, tarred roof. Inside, the shed was sectioned off for the individual bins to sit in. It always smelled damp and mossy, and was littered with cigarette butts where the big boys went for a fly fag.

We had collected dock leaves and succulent grasses from the scrubby back green behind our flats. We'd gathered up the leaves for Mrs Johnston, whose children Linda and Angus had a sad looking rabbit in a hutch near the washing poles. I felt sorry for the rabbit and had encouraged Morag to join me in foraging for greenery for its supper.

Morag usually did what I told her. She was a year younger than me, and a painfully quiet girl who lived in the flat below ours with her older sister and her parents. I'd left a note with the leaves, which read, cryptically, From The Helping Hands. I used a stub of red crayon, which now had so little paper left on it that I had no more to rip off. Soon, I'd need to begin using the yellow and pink crayons which I didn't like so much, but would have to last until I got a new box in my Christmas stocking. Acquiring the paper was easier. My father was a teacher and used to bring home odds and ends of scrap paper, ripped from old jotters, with one side scored or written on. Most children liked getting sweets or toys, but I liked gifts of writing materials. My eyes widened hopefully when he unfastened his brief case and pulled out a wad of assorted blank paper, sometimes written on one side. Occasionally there were stubs of pencils too. Bounty indeed.

Now, Morag and I were waiting for Mrs Johnston to bring in her washing, which flew on the line in the chilly autumn afternoon. The washing was getting a good blow, as they say in Edinburgh, but was also being speckled with grey flakes of soot from the chimneys of the blocks of flats where we lived.

Mrs Johnston, like most of the other women living in the flats, did her best, I realised, even as a small child. She always dispirited, and generally wore an expression similar to the rabbit, I thought. I felt sorry for her, and for the rabbit, and the children in the family. I wanted Mrs Johnston to acknowledge my good deed, though. I was a Brownie, after all, and we were supposed to help other people. Burnishing up my badge each week with a tiny amount of Brasso, I fervently tried to live up to the motto. I loved being a Brownie, putting on my uniform every Tuesday evening, struggling with the daffodil yellow scarf, and walking with my mother through the frosty night streets to the church hall where the rest of the pack assembled.

I was in the Pixie patrol, and invented many stories which involved me becoming tiny at will and being able to remain concealed in the grass where I met with insects and butterflies, as well as fairies and gnomes. This magical kingdom was a cross between toy town in the Enid Blyton books, and a fairy land as depicted in the Ladybird books.

I kept hoping that I'd be able to put my Brownie skills to use one day. Perhaps a lady with a broken arm would need my scarf as a temporary sling until the ambulance arrived? Or maybe I could darn socks and save my mother doing it? She wouldn't let me of course, I wasn't good enough.

This kindliness didn't extend to my sister, of course, with whom I shared a room. I certainly wouldn't help her in any way, she was child subject to frequent ear and chest infections, who demanded and received a lot of attention from my mother.

"I'm fed up lying here, Mary," whined Morag." It's cold and I'm bored. Let's go inside and play with our dolls. My granny has knitted a new frock and cardigan for Rosebud, she looks so nice in it!"

"No, we're staying here till Mrs Johnston comes out!" I said sternly. Morag's lower lip began to tremble faintly and I saw the first teardrop forming in her watery blue eyes.

"We'll go in five minutes," I said, confident that as neither of us had a watch, she would rely on me to know when five minutes had gone. But I knew time was limited and felt my power over her slipping away.

Just then, the close back door creaked open and Mrs Johnston emerged carrying an old tin bath and proceeded to take her washing off the line. She glanced at the hutch and looked more closely when she saw the note. I moved on the shed roof, ostentatiously, making sure she saw me. She smiled and nodded before trudging back across the scrubby grass. Morag tugged at my sleeve." Can we go in now, Mary?"

"You go," I said imperiously. "I'll wait here a bit." I was writing one of my dramatic and blood thirsty plays for the children in the stair to perform and knew I could get peace here, away from Sandra and also away from my mother asking me to tidy my half of the bedroom or do my homework. "Make sure you do your homework!" was her constant mantra. Even at eight, I had figured out that our family was an oddity. My father was a teacher, we lived amongst books and my parents bought The Observer on a Sunday, but we were living in a rented council flat in a working class area. They sent me across the city to a private girls' school but looking back, I realised that they could only afford it because the school was subsidised by the city corporation and I'd passed the highly competitive entrance exam which gave me what was in those days a golden key to elite education.

The explanation of this contradictory situation was easily understood by me as an adult: my parents had married very young, while he was still a student, and had two children in quick succession. At that point, dad had only been working for a couple of years and they weren't able to buy a house, as they later did.

Morag clambered down from the roof and ran for the close door, shouting, "See you after!" I glanced up to see her thin, pale legs with their crumpled ankle socks disappearing inside the heavy door.

I got out my pencil and some sheets of graph paper, this week's haul of discarded school supplies, and began to write. I was in the middle of writing a very gripping drama where two lords would fight to the death in a bloody duel, at the very gates of Edinburgh Castle, and watched by a huge crowd of onlookers. Although Lord Robert was the nicer person, I secretly preferred Sir Simon. I picture him in a metal breastplate and helmet with a plumed red feather. Sir Simon's shield was emblazoned with red dragon breathing fire and with a wild look in its green eyes, and his sword was bright and beautifully fashioned.

I longed for armour with a hunger which was completely illogical. My cousin Thomas, who was two years older than me, and lived in a bungalow in Milton Road, had a fantastic set of grey plastic armour which I seriously coveted. It had an embossed breast plate which buckled around the back, a sword and scabbard and best of all, a helmet with a visor and a plumed feather.

When I went to play at his house, he let me wear the armour and play with his toy castle. I envied his collection of toy knights on horseback who duelled with long spears and lances. He also had toy princesses and maids, which stood on the battlements of the castle, looking on as the knights duelled down below.

I had asked my mother for a castle for Christmas one year, but got a doll's house instead. Still, that was good too, because the dolls who lived in the house had an interesting existence and many adventures, under my supervision. One play I'd written involved the dolls hiding a fugitive knight in their coal cellar. He was so pleased with their help that he gave them his plumed helmet as a keepsake.

Shuffling into a more comfortable position on the bucket shed roof, I began to write.

Sir Simon de Fury: "Draw your weapon and fight me, you fucking bastard!" Waving sword. "I will have your black heart on a spike at the Castle before night is nigh!"

Lord Robert de Lancelot: "Pray spare me, sire!" Falls to knees. I heard words from the other children round about where I lived which I didn't hear at school. Pig was a big insult at my school. These other words seemed better though, more fitting for warring knights, somehow. I heard Graham from number seven shouting these words just the other day when his pal grabbed his packet of fags and ran up the street with them.

I was aware, without even looking up, that someone had hauled open the close door in the next block of flats. There was a scraping noise as the heavy wooden door, slightly swollen with damp, was pulled open.

"There she is, the poor aristocrat!"

I'd hoped they hadn't seen me. My body tensed and I kept my head down low near the paper, writing steadily, trying to contain the tremble of my hand.

Sir Simon de Fury:" Get up, you cowardly bugger and fight me like a man, not a big Jessie!"

Lord Robert de Lancelot: "But I have already lost a lot of blood and am too weak to fight…"

"Thinks she's better than us, going to that fancy school. Big snob, big snob!"

The chanting began and I'd no choice but to look up. Jennifer Wilson, a small, sneering girl with a mass of wiry ginger hair and a dirty cardigan led the shouting from the other side of the chain link fence which separated her back green from mine. A couple of boys had stopped kicking their football about and stood behind her. To my dread, I noticed that her older sister Beryl was also in the back green. Jennifer was a mouthy brat, but Beryl was really a nasty piece of work.

I hadn't actually done anything to them, they just didn't like me being at another school, and they shunned me from their street games of hopscotch and skipping. "Fuck off back to your ain hoose", Beryl said when I tried to join in with them.

Very slowly and carefully, I gathered up the papers and crayons and climbed down from the shed roof. My feet were almost on the ground when the first stone hit my shoulder. Nothing for it but to duck and run, I thought, I was a cowardly bugger just like Lord Robert de Lancelot. The second stone missed me by inches and I paused in flight, just for a second.

"Get the stuck up wee bitch!" shouted Beryl.

What happened next was over in a few seconds. One of the boys launched a half-brick in my direction, just as Jennifer half-turned her head towards her sister. The missile, intended for me, struck Jennifer on the temple and without even a scream, she fell backwards onto the muddy grass.

The silence was eerie, the children in the other green seemed incapable of moving for the interminable seconds it took before Beryl began screaming, a hideous keening, primitive, coming from her gut, not her throat.

Chapter Six *The Institute of Correction*

I laid out my possessions on the thin mattress covering the iron framed bed and watched a solitary tear drop from my cheek onto my precious little pile of scrap paper. Conscious that the other girls in the dormitory were watching me, I quickly put away my clothes in the scarred wooden cupboard and made up my bed with the rough sheets. Now what?

One of the other girls shifted from her bed and came to stand beside me.

"What did you dae, then?" she asked, getting straight to the point.

"I...I was found guilty of killing a girl by hitting her with a brick. But I didn't do it. It was Brian Kelly. The other kids ganged up on me, said it was me."

The girl shifted her thin body from one foot to the other, and folded her arms, laughing unpleasantly. The look in her wary green eyes, set in a pinched, sharp face, was hostile. "Aye right, and ah didnae set fire to our school either. A big boy did it an' ran away!"

I faced her. "My dad has got me a lawyer and I'll be out of here soon," I said, my lip trembling.

The girl laughed again. "Yeah, they all say that too!"

I have to just get through this and out the other side, I thought. Even at eight, I could see what had simply to be endured. The food was stodgy, the bed uncomfortable and the schooling from the teachers who came into the home was lacklustre. I could feel myself slipping back mentally, my brain seemed clouded in a permanent fog and my usually vivid imagination was dim and dull. The lack of a steady flow of reading and writing materials was the biggest deprivation for me, and I also realised that most of the other girls, even those of my age, were way behind me in reading, writing and sums.

The worst thing though, was my parents and sister visiting every Sunday. My dad looked grey and old, my mother and sister close to tears throughout the hour long visit. My mother told me on one visit that dad had a new job at a school in Perthshire, and that they would be moving away from Edinburgh soon.

Her face worked hard not to show how upset she was as she described their new house, "in a little village, very near the countryside, it will be lovely for you when… when all this is over!" she said brightly.

"Is this a head of job for you, dad?" I asked.

He hesitated a moment, then looked out of the window of the visitors room where we all sat on uncomfortable chairs, trying to behave normally.

"Well, not exactly, Mary," he said. "It's what we call a sideways move, I'll just have the same job teaching maths and it's a smaller school, so the salary is a little less."

I sat motionless, my face stiffening as I tried not to cry.

"On the bright side, Mary, the price of housing is much cheaper where we are going than in Edinburgh, so we've been able to buy a cottage with three bedrooms, so you and Sandra can have your own bedrooms at last!" His smile didn't reach his eyes, I noticed. "There's a garden, too, for you to play in, and a school for Sandra in the village, no travelling for her!"

I stared at him. "But what about your head of job, dad? And won't you miss Edinburgh, the shops, the red buses, the pictures, all the things we have there? How will you get to work if there are no buses?" Dad cleared his throat. My mother was dabbing her eyes with a hanky and Sandra was weeping openly. "I'm learning to drive and we'll have a car soon," my dad said, in a brisk tone. "There may be opportunities in this new school, or others in the area, for me to be a head of department eventually."

He took my hand, an unusual move as we weren't a tactile family, and looked me straight in the eye.

"A terrible things has happened to you, Mary, a dreadful injustice. I've spoken to a lawyer but he feels there is no real basis for an appeal. You have to sit it out here as best you can, and your family will be there when you get out. We are moving to give you, and ourselves, a fresh start away from wagging tongues and bad memories. It will all work out in the end, you'll see."

I managed to contain my tears until they were leaving, when my mother gave me a hug and asked what colour I'd like my room painted. Dad handed me a pile of scrap paper and some pencils, but the member of staff sitting a little apart from us and supervising the visit shook her head quietly and he reluctantly stowed them back in his briefcase. "Keep thinking, keep imagining, keep writing stories in your head, Mary", dad whispered as he kissed my cheek. "No-one can lock up your brain."   I could cope with most things at the home, I learned not to miss sweets and tasty meals; I got used to the uncomfortable bed and the lack of privacy sharing a dormitory with other girls that I didn't know. The cruelty of the other children and their sneering at my posh voice didn't affect me because that's how it had been at home too. It was all just so unfair, that I was here at all.

"Are you sure that Brian threw the brick which killed Jennifer?" The sheriff had asked me several times over at the court. I kept telling him that I hadn't lifted a stone, instead, I was running away from the children who were throwing stones at me. But it was my word against that of three other children. One by one, Brian Kelly, his friend Robert Scott, and the horrible Beryl trooped into the high wooden witness box and told their lies. Three against one, their stories were pat. They said that I didn't like Jennifer, and that I had deliberately flung the brick which killed her. Put like that, it was simple and straightforward, really.

I watched Brian Kelly give his evidence. Wearing a Fair Isle pullover, a grey shirt and his school tie and with his hair slicked back with water, he looked and sounded convincing. "She doesnae like us, she's posh and says big words. We were just mucking aboot, kicking a ball in the green, when she started her shouting, then she picked up a big brick and flung it right at Jennifer," he said. "Then there wis blood pouring from Jennifer's heid, an' she fell richt doon on the grass," he added, ghoulishly. A doctor read from his notes, saying that the child Jennifer Wilson had been brought to the Infirmary by ambulance, but despite their best efforts to save her, she had died a few hours after her arrival at the hospital. A post mortem examination showed she had been killed by a blow to her temple from a heavy object. He agreed that a half brick or similar could have been the weapon.

I was eight. I'd reached the age of criminal responsibility.

There wasn't an option but to send me off to the reformatory.

Chapter Seven *Injustice*

Wariness. That's how I was, always, with everyone.
At the school I went to, far away from Edinburgh. The
reformatory at least did me that one favour, they let me keep
up with my education.

"We've decided to help you, Mary. We're going to send you
up to Dundee."
Miss Matheson looked at me over her spectacles, her
corrugated grey hair unmoving as she held my gaze.
"You are a bright girl and can go to a good school up there
where no-one will know you. I believe your parents have
moved away from Edinburgh: Perthshire, isn't it?"

My cheeks flushed hot and sore. My mother, taken away
northwards, away from her friends, her city. My father,
leaving the school he loved, and where he had hoped to
become head of, had gone to teach instead in a mediocre
secondary school. My sister had faced a big upheaval too: a
new school for her as well, all her friends left behind. All
because of me. All because of Brian Kelly and the other
children.

It all passed, eventually. The pain diminished, gradually, although the feeling of injustice and helplessness never left me.

I did well at my new school, going as a day pupil to an excellent school in Dundee. At night, I returned to the institution. It meant that I always had to make excuses when girls in my class asked me home for tea. I knew I could never reciprocate, so I always refused, on one pretext or another. Of course, eventually I was allowed home at weekends, and when I was 14, I was finally released from the institution. I'd served my time, it was all over. I continued at the school in Dundee, boarding during the week and going home to my parents at weekends. A couple of years later, I gained my Highers and headed back to Edinburgh, to university.

It was a fresh start, but I was changed utterly.

Friends, lovers, acquaintances and fellow students all said the same about me.

"You're deep, aren't you? You don't give much away!"

No-one ever got close, I made sure of that. I was very careful always to deflect, fudge and ignore awkward questions. Being so closed off meant that I protected my privacy, but it also led to emotional isolation, and loneliness.

Chapter Eight *University*

"Look out! There's a desk in the way!"

The young man standing before me had black curly hair and a
cheeky grin, which widened as he steadied me from falling. In
a dream as usual, I nearly went smack into the edge of the
desk in the University library.

There followed coffee, an exchange of history – with mine
firmly edited of course – and before long, Alan and I were an
item. As the time went by, I began to relax more with him,
and was less cagey. Apart, of course, from the information
locked away in the box in my head, labelled Jennifer Wilson,
and the deeper, stranger secrets of the child I'd been in
previous incarnations.

We were both reaching the end of third year at this point, with
our final, honours year to complete before graduation. The
summer drifted by, with its golden days, bright evenings,
giving us some time to read for pleasure, to see friends, and to
save some money for next term's books. Alan had a job as a
labourer on a building site and I got vacation work in a coffee
bar. We saw each other when we could – difficult, as he
worked all day and I began work at 5pm – and fell exhausted
into bed each night, usually at my tiny flat in Newington.

Unusually, I didn't share with other students, having decided that I wanted uninterrupted peace to study without the distractions of other flatmates around. There was a cost involved, but I worked in term-time to pay for the luxury. And of course, it was still the halcyon days of student grants…

"Here you go!" Alan said one night in the pub, carefully lifting a glass of gin and tonic from this shirt pocket, and setting down the pints on the scarred wooden table. Our friends were all around, chatting, laughing, sharing packets of crisps, and looking with concentration through the jobs section in the Guardian.

"What wage-slave occupation are you planning then, Alan?" Joe had a half-sneer on his face which made me want to punch him. He was a champagne socialist who went on CND marches and wore clothes which were both torn and dirty. Joe's beard was started in the first term of his first year studying history and politics, and had grown over four years along with his fake anti-establishment views.

"Well, I've always wanted to teach, so I'll be doing the year at teacher training college before I can be gainfully employed!" Alan spoke easily, but I felt the simmering anger beginning in him, and a heat from where his shoulder touched mine on the crowded bench. "Ha! Throwing pearls before wee swine for the rest of your life," snorted Joe, glugging down his beer.

"What are you going to do then?" asked Alan, quietly.

"Oh, I dunno." Joe fumbled in his shirt pocket and pulled out a scarred tobacco tin. As he made a roll-up, he said: "I'm not doing what you do, anyway, getting into a system where I have to doff my cap to some master and take my pittance at the end of the month, that's for sure."

What happened next was so swift, so sudden, and so unexpected that we all sat as if paralysed. One moment we were all sitting around the table; the next, Joe was flat on his back on the floor, groaning, with his nose spurting blood. Alan was crouched over Joe, gripping a huge fold of greasy flannel shirt in both hands.

"You unspeakable little shit!" he yelled.

I'd never seen Alan so angry. His face was red, and the hands locked onto Joe's shirt were bone-white. There was a silence in the pub, broken only by Alan's voice.

"How dare you mock me for wanting, having to make a living! You are a waste of space, a leech. You kid on to be some sort of rebel, criticising everyone who works, while you sit on your fucking arse knowing daddy will always bail you out!"

There was a gasp around the table, as if Alan' words had released us from the paralysed state. Joe's father and the family fortune was a taboo subject. Very few people knew that Joe's family were wealthy, fabulously so. Joe came from a background of inherited wealth, old money, made from the tobacco trade. Alan had found out by chance when he accidentally picked up and read Joe's opened bank statement from the hall of the flat they shared with two other students. "Bloody hell, Joe, that's a load of dosh in your account," he'd joked, but Joe was angry.

"Don't you ever tell anyone about that," he warned. But Alan, wisely or not, had persisted with him and the truth emerged. Joe had no need of a grant, or a holiday job, or any job at all. He was, literally, the idle rich.

"Right lads, that's it over, whatever it was," said Mike, the bar manager. "Take it outside, or better still, stop it right now," he said, a frisson of weariness in his voice. How many more fights would he have to break up, how many more broken beer glasses to sweep up? Oh, thought Mike, oh, how good it would be to have a peaceful, friendly little bar in Spain, where his customers would be white haired, beringed pensioners who chatted about their grandchildren and how much money they were saving on heating by spending the winter in Benidorm.

Mike helped a stunned Joe to his feet, set the bench back upright and returned to washing up glasses behind the bar.

Our friends were embarrassed by the scene. One by one, they drifted away, outside into early summer evening. Joe muttered something under his breath, then headed off through the pub door, still dabbing his bleeding nose.
Alan and I sat alone, not speaking for a bit.

"That was brave, but also very stupid of you," I said. "Brave to speak up, to put Joe in his place and show him up for the hypocrite he is. Stupid, though, because now you'll need to look for another place to stay. I don't think Joe will want you as a flatmate after this."
That's how Alan and I came to live together.

Alan stayed that night at my flat, as he had many times before. Next day, he collected together his clothes, books and record collection brought them in a taxi – a rare luxury - and installed himself in my space. Without a real choice being made, without any real declarations of feelings, or any firm thought for the future, we moved into this new part of our relationship.
It seemed the next logical step for Alan to meet my parents.

"Is that alright then, if I bring Alan home to meet you?"
As always, the conversations with my mother were stilted.
They always had an edge to them, an unspoken sub-text. The
past was past, but it still impacted on everyday life.

 "Well yes, Mary. Of course you must bring your friend to
meet us. Come on Sunday for lunch. Oh and Mary, does he
know anything about…" she tailed off, and I could picture her
fingering her pearls nervously, and glancing round to see if
my father or Sandra was in earshot.
"No, mother, he doesn't know anything about Jennifer
Wilson, if that's what you mean. I've told him we lived in
Edinburgh, and moved to Perthshire when I was eight. He
knows where dad teaches, and also about me going to school
in Dundee. All is fine, you don't need to fret."
I kept my voice calm, but I could feel the old familiar
sensation of blood rushing into my face, then draining away
just as fast. And the sick, horrible churning in my stomach
which landed there every time I was forced to think about
Jennifer Wilson. Like some ghastly memento, a hideous,
unwanted souvenir, the image of the child lying motionless on
the ground of scrubby back green, the brick lying at her head
and blood soaking the sparse grass, came easily into my mind.
I closed my eyes to blot it out, and felt dizzy.

"Are you still there, Mary?" my mother was asking.

"Yes, of course. We'll catch the early train up on Sunday: can dad meet us at the station? Oh, Sandra will? Of course, I forgot she was sitting her driving test this week. That's great she passed first time!"

The conversation flowed easily now, onto the mundane, the small coinage of life in my family living a rural Perthshire village. We talked of how Sandra's first year at teacher training college was going, the WRI sponge cake competition, and the unwelcome reduction of the village bus service. As we moved onto these safe topics, I could picture my mother relaxing at the other end of the phone.

She could have been so bitter about the diminishing of her life, the hauling up of her cherished roots from the city she loved so well. Instead, she made the best of the circumstances, embedded in the new community, and tried to live for the moment, and for the future. But it was always there, this lurking blackness from the past, the shadow across the sun.

"So you're planning to be a teacher, Alan?" my father said, a little too cheerfully. He actually rubbed his hands in some kind of phony jollity.

Alan answered thoughtfully, all the while cutting up the beef and roast potatoes on his plate.

"Well, I'd like to make a difference to young people, to help them get a good start in life, encourage their interest and enthusiasm. Hopefully, fire up their wish to know more about the delights of chemistry!"

My father smiled. "Yes, nothing quite like seeing a pupil really get the bit between their teeth and get to grips with your subject!"

Trying too hard, dad, I thought, and you're mixing metaphors here. Keeping things normal, I suppose. Keeping things light, in the present.

Lunch passed unremarkably enough. With one practising teacher and two education students at the table, it was an easy conversational route. Once or twice there were brief silences, when Alan innocently asked where dad had taught, and why he's left Edinburgh to teach in rural Perthshire.

Mother answered that one, after a quick, sideways glance at her husband."Oh, well, John had been looking for a head of department's post for a while, and this one came up. It meant we could move out of the flat we were in, not the nicest of neighbourhoods in Edinburgh." Alan's thick silence had descended, and was palpable. One thing he simply couldn't stand was social snobbery.

Mother hurried on: "We liked the countryside and the rural area and we felt it was better for the girls. Sandra's bad chest, you know, fresher air… and John and I so love the garden here!"

There, that was it over and done with, the story told, all the wee inconsistencies smoothed over like fresh plaster on a trowel covering up cracks in a ceiling. We were the perfect family once more.

After lunch, everyone seemed to relax a little, and mother asked Alan about his family.

He had a natural wit, ironic and amusing and he soon had us all laughing at his stories.

"My little sisters, well, not so little now, they are 18, are just a nightmare," he said, smiling. "They're identical twins and are up to all sorts of nonsense. They pretend to be each other and have even gone on dates with poor unsuspecting blokes, making out they are the other twin!"

We laughed at his description of his father, who ran his own joinery business and was never seen without a stub of pencil behind his ear.

"He once went to the barber's after a bit of a gap since his last haircut, so his hair was longer than usual. He almost had the pencil snipped in two, the barber only noticed it at the last minute," said Alan, ruefully. "My mother just despairs of him. He's too nice a person to be a big business tycoon, that's for sure. He's always 'just fixing' things for the people who can't afford to pay much, and comes home with cakes and bags of vegetables in lieu of cash. Once, he was given a kitten in payment for fixing an old lady's shed door! My mum wasn't too pleased, I can tell you!"

Chapter Nine *Beginnings and Endings*

Funny how familiarity, inertia, the mundanity of daily life takes over, and removes, suppresses, the ability to make real decisions. I never really asked myself if I truly loved Alan, or what love was, in fact. We were largely compatible, we got along, and we wanted roughly the same things: careers, a home and a family.

We were happy enough, though, and somehow we slid into an engagement. To my horror, looking back, I can't actually remember Alan proposing, it just came up in the middle of a conversation about where we planned to find jobs, and well, we were then engaged. We did choose a ring together, from a velvet tray in the window of an old antique shop down near the Grassmarket. It was an old Victorian silver band, set with emeralds.

"Oh, you aren't superstitious then?" said my sister when she saw the ring. "Wearing an engagement ring which someone has had in the past, and might have had an unhappy marriage?" I just smiled, and said nothing.

We married once we graduated and started our jobs. Alan, as he planned, became a chemistry teacher at one of Edinburgh's secondary schools, while I began my indentureship as a graduate trainee journalist with a group of local weekly papers. We stayed in my rented flat for a while, but we quickly planned to have our own home.

"Hey, this is nice!" said Alan, as we viewed a flat to buy in Tollcross. It was small, the decoration dated back to VE day and the kitchen consisted of a badly chipped, deep Ulster sink, over which was a gas geyser for hot water, and an ancient stove which looked like it was held together with rust. The previous owner had died, we guessed, because there were still some old pieces of furniture here and there.
"The furniture and all fitments are included in the sale price," enthused the estate agent who was showing us around the flat.
"Is that good or bad?" I whispered to Alan, and we both giggled.
We bought the flat, which was antiquated but centrally situated, so we didn't need to buy a car. Alan's father performed joinery miracles, not least in the kitchen, which was soon transformed into a light, bright room with shelves and cupboards, and a modern sink and cooker.

Not long before we moved permanently into the flat, I went there one day to clean away the remains of sawdust and hang curtains. Alan was refereeing a football match at the youth club where he volunteered, so I was alone. I had just finished hanging up the bright yellow curtains at the kitchen window, when I glanced down, watching the Saturday crowds thronging the streets.

To my surprise, I saw a small group of people in old fashioned costumes making their way slowly up towards the Meadows. Must be fringe performers, I thought, then looked more closely, and saw that they were walking right through the stream of pedestrians, and were attracting no glances.
It was Morningside Mary, with her governess and her older sister Elizabeth. I'd seen them all before, a number of times over the years, but there was something different this time. Attached to the group, but hanging back a little, part of it but separate, was another young woman, my age, in modern clothes. She was small and slightly built, with short, blonde hair. She was standing motionless, her arms folded across her chest. She raised her head and looked up at me. My heart gave a staggering, frightening, glorious leap inside me. The connection between us fizzed bright and true in the dull afternoon, a lightning bolt, an anchoring, and a certainty.

This was the other person, then. This was our story, this was our journey together beginning, starting, decades before we would meet properly. Then she vanished, an abrupt disappearance.

I looked harder at the little group on the pavement. Mary then raised her head, almost in slow motion, and hung back a little from her governess and her sister. She looked straight up at me, her face its usual pale colour, and her bright red curls peeping from under her velvet beret. She stared so long, so hard that the energy from her struck the pane of glass with tangible thud. She locked onto me in a way she'd never done before: my better connection had always been with High Street Mary.

"Beware, be careful," Mary said to me, her little voice insistent in my ear. From nowhere, from somewhere inside me, I said back to her: "Don't do it, Mary. Please don't do it."

Then she was gone, away. Miss Hamilton and Elizabeth had vanished too. The street still thronged with shoppers, maroon buses trundled along, a flower seller shouted his wares, bundling dripping irises, fresh from their bucket of water, into paper cones for his customers. I sat for a long time in the newly re-covered chair by the gas fire, my cheeks wet with tears. Found, and lost again, instantly. The happiness deferred till an unknown time, if ever it was to be.

A voice behind me whispered: "Wait. Be strong. It will be."
I whirled round just in time to catch a glimpse of Aunt Jessie,
fading into the newly painted walls. I lit a cigarette, the first
that day, as Alan and I were both trying to stop smoking. My
hand shook as I flicked the lighter. If there had been a bottle of
gin handy, without a doubt I'd have been pouring a large
glass.

The marriage was, well, as well as it could be, when I hid and
concealed so much.

Many decades later, Princess Diana was to say that there were
three people in her marriage. In mine, there were so many
other people, as well as the huge secret of my years at the
approved school, there was so little room for Alan and me as a
real couple. We worked together on the practicalities of
building a home, moving from the Tollcross flat to a terraced
villa in Willowbrae just before Phoebe was born. Steven
followed a couple of years later. Life took on a pattern, not
exciting, but familiar.

I fitted some freelance work around the childcare, while Alan
moved up through the teaching ranks, ending up as head of
department.

It got so Alan and I said very little to each other. In the evenings, once the children were in bed, he usually had marking to do, unless he was at the many parents' nights or other after-school activities with which he was involved. Highlight of our week was a bottle of wine and a carry-out Chinese meal on a Saturday night, while we watched Casualty and checked our lottery numbers.

We weren't unique, of course. Millions of couples like us throughout the country.

I found out about Alan's affair in such a clichéd way: emptying his suit pockets for debris before I took it to the dry cleaners. It was just a tiny thing, but so revealing. A condom, tucked deep in an inside pocket. I had been sterilised after Steven's difficult birth, so it certainly wasn't intended for me.

"Why? Why?" I said through tears that night when he came whistling in the front door, late as usual, after a meeting at work. Well, he wasn't the first man to have used the 'meeting after work' excuse to spend time with his lover, and he sure as hell wouldn't be the last…

The colour dropped out of his face as if someone had turned off a tap. It was his eyes though that chilled me. They were furtive, darting, like those of an animal cornered.

I sat at the kitchen table and reached again for the open wine bottle. My hand shook as I refilled my glass and poured one for him.

Like a burst paper bag, he seemed to have had all the energy sucked from him. He sat down, his eyes still flickering around the room. At last, his gaze settled on the spice rack, a foot or so above my head.

He gulped down the glass of wine in one swallow before speaking.

"I don't know, I can't tell you. It just happened. She's a new member of staff, of my department. I've had to help her settle in, give her some advice..." His voice weakened and halted. Not a stupid man, he knew how pathetic this sounded once the words hit the air. He kept his eyes firmly fixed on the jar of mixed herbs, as if his life depended upon it.

I drank some more wine and sat quietly for a few moments. The silence was thick and heavy, a malevolent blanket suffocating us. A sudden calm came over me, and I felt able to talk rationally to him.

"Is it serious? Do you love her?"

The words sat in the air, hovering, like malevolent insects.

"I, I don't know. I can't leave you anyway. The children, the house…" again he tailed off, not sure what to say. I realised with sudden and utter certainty that he didn't love me. He just didn't want a lot of upset and disruption in his life, which a split between us would inevitably bring.

I also acknowledged to myself that I didn't love him either and probably never had. I was, of course, eventually going to find out exactly what it was like to truly love somebody. Three people, in succession, over the space of several years, but despite my compelling knowledge of my life in the previous three centuries, I was unable to see into the future. It was all very frustrating.

That evening, sitting across from Alan and watching the carefully-constructed family edifice start to crumble, I didn't know what was going to happen later, any more than he did. I had to ask the question."What do you want to do?" I asked Alan, with only the slightest cracking in my voice. "Don't you love me?" He looked like a cornered rat, which was exactly what I thought of him at that moment. I let the silence deepen until it became almost intolerable to bear, like a heavy, cloying weight descending over us again. Suddenly, Alan lowered his eyes to meet mine, looking at me properly, for the first time since he came in.

"I don't know you!" he burst out. "You are like an ice maiden! There is no warmth about you, you are cold and closed off, secretive, aloof. We don't laugh about anything, I don't know what you really feel or think. I can't connect with you, there's always been this mystery, I can't get close .If only you would let go a bit, let me in, and trust me properly. Maybe we could have been closer, better together."

He sighed, and glanced at me. I sat, my face graven, unmoving. He needed to talk, I let him. It was easier anyway, meant he could rant and I could just sit listening.

"Even when we are closest, when we make love… you aren't there. You are somewhere else, unattainable, closed off. We lie inches apart in bed together, and I sometimes feel like we could be on opposite sides of the Grand Canyon."

He took a slug of wine, and continued. Now the dam had burst, there was no stopping him, it seemed.

"Carole loves me. She cares about me. She confides in me, she listens to me, she understands my frustrations. I listen to her, too. I know her, she's open to me, and there aren't secrets, silences, no-go areas between us. She's warm, tactile, loving, caring. She puts little notes in my pigeonhole at school, sometimes just a heart drawn with kisses… or she leaves a Walnut Whip on my desk."

His face softened as he spoke.

"To her, I'm a man, not just a meal ticket who pays the mortgage…"

He heard my gasp and stopped.

"Yes, I know you earn as much as me and pay the bills too," he said. "But I feel like a bloody robot."

He sighed and poured more wine, emptying the bottle. He glanced round for a second and I knew what he was thinking: is there another bottle? Strange how I knew him so well. Or thought I did, anyway.

Reassured by the sight of a full bottle of red, uncorked and breathing on the dresser, he continued.

"Carole makes me feel like a person again, not just someone who takes Phoebe to dance classes or Steven to football practice, who cuts the grass every fortnight and spends Sunday evening with a pile of marking. We don't have any fun!" he concluded.

A childish, selfish brat of a man, I suddenly thought. My second thought was: why on earth did I ever get married?

Of course he's right. I am closed off, and he knows it. There's so much about me he doesn't know, and never can.

He talked for hours, and I mostly listened. Not much I could say, really, except to defend my position as a good wife and mother, equal breadwinner and upholder of the family, who also wanted more freedom than I had.

"Mid-life crisis," I thought, as he continued to complain about my emotional barrenness and reproached me for my shortcomings as a lover, a wife, a soul-mate.

But, in fairness, he had a point or two. I felt worried, angry, cheated, let down, disgusted and betrayed. Of course I did. But the little voice in my head, the Jiminy Cricket conscience where we all know the truth, said: "You, and your circumstances, are to blame. You could never have had a normal life, who are you kidding? You expected Alan to be content with the emotional crumbs from your table, and now you are complaining because he's found someone to give him the whole loaf? Harsh, but fairly accurate, Jiminy.

There wasn't any drama after that night, as it happened. We eventually went to bed, both quite drunk, but not at the swirling of the room or nausea stage, and managed to lie, not touching, at either side of the mattress. As I fell into a dreamless sleep, I thought, incongruously, how lucky it was that we had chosen to buy such a large bed, so there was no danger of us touching by accident.

Having said his piece, he agreed to end it with Carole, although said he had to keep seeing her at work.

We patched things up and carried on more or less as before. I tried, he tried, but I knew about the crumbling cliff-edge we stood upon.

Chapter Ten *The School Project*

We might have staggered along till old age except for the school project. The first flutterings of fear landed on me one afternoon in the autumn. Always my favourite time of year, when the city trees die back to golden yellow and the late afternoon air turns smoky with the breaths of people waiting at bus stops. I'd been working at home, writing up a particularly difficult interview from the day before. The interviewee, a city landlord, had proved hostile, evasive and truculent. I tried to elicit, fairly, his side of a story which was going to make unhappy reading for him, in a day's time through the medium of the paper for which I worked. His tenants, many of them, had spilled the beans about the conditions in which they lived, which frankly beggared belief. I was waiting for a comment from the council's press office regarding environmental health's involvement in the case, and was also prepared for the story to collapse instantly if criminal charges were brought and the matter became *sub judice.*

I knew the signs, of course, when interviewing the nasty bit of work of a landlord. Who better than me, who has spent all this time concealing, obscuring, hiding, lying and covering up the truth, to recognise a fellow traveller on the road? I had turned again to my notes just as Phoebe rattled open the heavy front door and called to me.

"Hi mum, guess what we are doing at school? Our family history! Cool, eh?" She stood before me, pulling off her jacket and school scarf, her lovely auburn curls tangled, misted with moisture. My lovely girl, everything I always wanted. As a small child, her hair was like thistledown, refusing to be constrained by slides, ribbons or grips. I loved her and her brother so much.

She chatted with all the enthusiasm of a 14 -year-old who relishes the newness of each day, who anticipates the joyful experiences ahead for her. "… and we've to find out as much as we can about our ancestors, right back to olden times, like when you were a wee girl, mum! We're going to look at where everyone lived, what jobs they did, what life was like in Edinburgh." I would have smiled at this, but in my gut began the first churnings of disquiet. Like the first, early symptom of a disease you initially ignore, but eventually have to deal with, I recognised the flutter of danger.

Although my identity had been protected at the time of the court case, as I was only eight, journalists were present. The newspapers carried reports of the case, where I was known simply as Girl A. After my conviction, though, reporters talked to people round about in our housing scheme, including Jennifer's family, and it wasn't long before my name was known.

A Sunday tabloid broke the story, breaching the spirit of the law which protects minors, though staying legally just within its bounds. They called me Girl A again, but identified the approximate area of the city where I lived and also mentioned that I 'went to a posh school across the town', not the local primary school.

Before long, the family name was out there, and the details of our street, picked up by other reporters. I was then described as 'red-haired and stuck-up, with a terrible temper' by the neighbours.

I expect money changed hands, as people sold their story. Thirty pieces of silver would probably have been enough in those days to get people talking.

Of course, all this was kept from me at the time, as I started my years of punishment in the remand home. It was many years later that I pieced together the extent of the hell my parents must have endured in the aftermath of the court case.

I did what I could, to give her information for her project, as did her dad. Being a journalist came in handy, as at first I was able to direct her enquiries, give her safe material and pull her off course from the truth.

Looking in the bathroom mirror late one night, as the house and its inhabitants slept, I met my own gaze

"I hate this. I hate myself, my history, what has happened, the knowledge, the frustration, the fear," I whispered to my reflection. A pale-faced woman, her red hair dimmed and greying, with sad eyes, met my gaze.

The voice in my head said: "Surely you didn't expect this time to be different, did you?" Phoebe came home from school the next day, and I knew instantly there was something wrong. She closed the front door carefully, slowly and I heard her shoes tapping, dragging over the wooden entrance flooring, the sound muffled as she reached the patterned runner. I knew she'd been crying. There were still uneven streaks, like raindrops, on her freckled cheeks.

She sat down heavily on the kitchen chair. Just has her father had done a few years earlier, when I found out about Carole.

"Is it true, mum?" she said, unbuckling her bag and pulling out a sheaf of photocopied papers. "Is this you? Did you really kill a wee girl with a stone? And go to a reformatory?"

The photocopies of old newspaper cuttings fanned out on the pine table. I didn't need to turn them round to read the words. One skill I'd learnt as a young journalist in the final days of hot metal printing, was to be able to read the metal slugs of type in the wooden forms back to front and upside down, as the caseroom foreman tightened up the plates prior to printing. Incongruously, I suddenly saw myself back then leaning across the stone, with my long hair and miniskirt, knee high boots and careless thoughts, poring over the text with my by-line in italics.

I looked straight at Phoebe.

"Yes, I was found guilty of accidentally killing Jennifer Wilson, when I was eight. But I didn't do it, Phoebe. The other children ganged up on me because I was different from them. They lied. A boy threw the half brick which killed Jennifer." She looked at me as if I'd struck her across the face, then began to cry, with great, gulping sobs.

Of course I tried, to reason with Phoebe, to explain, but she was inconsolable. Alan was angry, upset and bewildered. I heard him on the 'phone to my father one evening, and he sounded cold and hard, almost unrecognisable, as he basically interrogated his father-in-law. I couldn't bear to hear the conversation, so I went upstairs and lay on my bed, weeping.

After a few days of this horrific situation, it seemed best that I leave home, although Steven decided he wanted to come with me.

I saw relief spattered across Alan's face when I told him I'd do this.

The revelation was the catalyst, the final straw –albeit more like a haystack – which he needed and wanted to end the farce of a marriage.

Phoebe stayed in her room the day I left, although I heard the faint noise of her crying as I left my house keys in the glass bowl on the hall settle.

Chapter Eleven *How to Reveal the Truth*

Because they've been clamouring at me, and because I know this is the last shot at it.

Because of natural justice.

Because I was upset at the dirty tricks used to get a No vote in the Referendum, another great injustice.

Because I wanted peace to live out my life, to die, and finish with it all.

Because I specially loved this set of children and the grandchildren I was able to see, Steven's two boys, and I didn't want to have to come back again, and find they had grown up and died.

Because the older grandson reminded me of me at seven, in this, the most recent of my lives.

Because the last time I met Alan, many years previously, at the solicitor's office to deal with final paperwork over the divorce and house sale, I noticed the changes which had already begun. He had taken off his wedding ring and exposed the white strip of skin below. Only a matter of time, and a couple of weeks' in Spain to even up the tan, and the waters would have closed there too. A finality. As if his finger had never been laden down with the married gold band.

He was wearing new clothes, too: a soft navy blue shirt with a matching tie, the top button undone to reveal a little chest hair and a very sparkling, new thin gold chain around his neck. I recognised the chain immediately for what it was – a gift from a new lover. Lacking the intimacy of a ring, or a watch, hidden and not on show, this was a gift bereft of the confidence that the relationship would last. But I knew that he'd clearly moved on with his life. I wondered if he'd gone back to Carole, or if this was someone new? The mild curiosity I felt confirmed my detachment from him. I should have been burning with jealousy, anger and hurt feelings.

But now, resolution had to come soon, before the new family patterns hardened forever and I was on the periphery for all time; before a new family script could be written where I was confined to a footnote in the margins of history.

 The Marys were clamouring, insisting that I act. They drifted into my dreams, and began appearing more frequently in my waking moments, wanting justice, fairness, and endings. Alan was polite, cool and utterly unforthcoming as we sat uncomfortably side by side in the solicitor's office, that last day, as we waited to settle the final practicalities of our dead marriage. "How's Phoebe?" I asked.

The ice formed in the air. He didn't turn to look at me, but just said: "She's fine. I'm looking after her and she will be ok."

"I'd like to see her sometime," I said, my voice sounding oddly faint and quavery.

"Not a good idea, Mary. She's been through enough already and is just starting to get settled in her new school. She doesn't want to see you anyway," he added, just the faintest tinge of smugness in his voice. She'd had to go to a new school.

Apparently, according to Alan, she's been so upset about the revelations that she felt unable to go back to her school, weighed down by the shameful knowledge which she couldn't ever share with her friends. Her mother was a murderer; her family was broken into pieces, and her beloved brother had gone too.

Phoebe's headmistress, Mrs Simmonds, needed to be told, of course. No doubt Alan just loved doing all that, spilling the beans and exposing my shameful past. He was the wronged husband, deceived and betrayed by his wife, and her family, all these years, living with someone, having children with them, not knowing the truth…

A few discreet phone calls had doubtless been made by Mrs Simmonds, connecting with others in the tight Edinburgh schools network. Arrangements had been made, and Phoebe had transferred to another school on the pretext of obscure subject timetabling availability, or a contrived but plausible health issue explaining the need to repeat a school year. All done without fuss, accommodations made, no doubt, everyone sweeping it all under the carpet till the rug is so high there is a visible bump.

Of course, I tried many times over the years to make contact with my daughter. I wrote, emailed, texted her, suggested meeting her in a neutral place, a coffee shop, at her grandparents' house, or with her brother, but to no avail. I heard from Steven now and then how she was faring. He gave me bits of odd, disjointed information, the way boys and men tell you things.

"Phoebe's left school and going to Uni, in Glasgow. "Phoebe got her degree. Some arty farty thing like interior design. Yeah, dad and Carole went to the graduation. Yep, I think dad and Carole are getting married, dunno when, though. They're buying a flat together, down at the waterfront in Granton. It's dead cool, all glass and chrome, brilliant view out to sea.

"Phoebe's got a flat in Glasgow, it's neat and there's loads of unusual furniture she got from old junk shops and fixed up and painted. Cameron put up a load of shelves for her and retiled the bathroom.

"Cameron? He's some bloke she met at Uni. Electronics engineer, works for that big IT outfit in Glasgow near the Merchant City, forget the name now… he's got a great car, an old Triumph Spitfire he's done up."

I had only one communication from Phoebe, an email, saying she was getting married to Cameron, changing her name and her email address, and didn't want me to keep emailing her, or writing letters for Steven to give to her. She didn't want anything to do with someone who had murdered a child, and then lied about it all the time. She used the phrase "lied by omission", it seemed so adult to me.

But then again, she was an adult now, and I had missed those precious growing up years as she went from teenager to young woman. She added that even if it had been an accidental murder, I still picked up the half brick intending to do Jennifer Wilson serious injury, and it was no excuse that I was a child myself.

"I've read all the old newspaper accounts, thought about it long and hard," Phoebe continued, in our first-ever, if one-sided, conversation on the topic.

"You were a child, I know, but you hated that girl enough to want to really damage her. Your temper, which we all have seen from time to time, must have driven you, I expect, and but that means you have it in you to lose your temper again. I hope that Cameron and I will have children one day, and I would never feel comfortable having you in their presence.

"Poor grandpa and grandma, and Auntie Sandra, had to move out of Edinburgh because of what you did. You married dad and told him nothing about this, he married an imposter! And then you went on to have me and Steven. Every day I think about what you did, have I inherited your temper, could I do such a thing, should I have children myself, just in case?

"I've been to see a counsellor at university and got a lot of it out there with her, and I've told Cameron everything when he asked me to marry him. I don't want my marriage and my family to start out with all these secrets and lies. Cameron says it was all a long time ago and doesn't mean I'm like you, so we have a clean slate to start our lives together.My tears were now uncontrollable and I had to stop reading for a few minutes.I poured a large whisky with no ice. Funnily enough, it's a drink I don't like and only keep in the house for making hot toddies, but it seemed the right thing to drink, the only thing fitting for that night.

I read on.

"So, I don't want you to ever contact me again. We will move out of Glasgow eventually, and have children, and a house and a cat or two, I expect. As far as anyone I meet from now on will know, I have a father and step-mother, Carole. If pressed, I'll say that my mother left many years ago and may well be dead, for all I know."

Later that night, in a whisky-induced haze, the crying finally ceased, and my tears faltered and stopped. I looked at myself in the bathroom mirror and saw a blotchy and red faced old woman with sad, terrible eyes looking at me.

The whisky did its work and I slept heavily, dry-mouthed, through the dream-laced night.

Chapter Twelve *Finding the Answers*

The woman at the Salvation Army office was sympathetic and helpful.

"A wrong was done a long time ago, and I need to find some people I knew as a child in Edinburgh," I told her. "Can you help me to trace them?"

She took some details, asked me to fill in some forms and to return in a week's time.

It was a typical, misty Edinburgh early autumn morning when I returned to the Salvation Army offices. I'd walked from my flat, noticing the sun beginning to burn through the clouds and the cobbles shimmering and steaming, glowing gold.

Walking through the old town, I glimpsed High Street Mary hovering in the mouth of a close, her legs pale below her skirt. She waved at me, and I smiled in her direction. A startled early morning tourist caught the benefit of my smile, and I turned away and hastened down the wakening street.

What had seemed a hopeless task suddenly began to appear do-able. The Salvation Army had been better in finding out the information than I could possibly have hoped.

There were three people who knew the truth about the death, apart from myself. Brian Kelly, Robert Scott and Beryl Wilson.

According to the Salvation Army's information, which was helpful but not complete, it appeared likely that at least two of the three people I sought were still alive, and they lived in the Edinburgh area, which was an astonishing bonus. At least there would be no extensive travelling involved, if these were indeed the same people. Beryl Wilson was proving the most difficult to trace, I guessed because she had married and changed her name.

I spent many weeks looking at newspaper archives, records of births, deaths and marriages at Register House. I Googled names, I walked around the city, looking, watching, remembering. Using the advice from the Salvation Army, I dug out articles, I researched. I visited the Central Library, I checked electoral registers, and I looked on Facebook and Twitter.

High Street Mary was around such a lot then, ducking in and out of the High Street closes and running past me on the cobbles of the High Street, her red hair flying behind her. She followed me into Greyfriars Kirkyard one day, where I sat on the grass looking at the notes from that morning's visit to the National Library. I heard a rustle in the grass, and I looked up, expecting to see a squirrel or even a bird nearby, looking for crumbs or a discarded apple core. City creatures are bolder than their country counterparts, coming close to humans, fearless. But this was no wild creature, just Mary, standing silently before me, her bare feet appearing to hover lightly over the cold ground.

She spoke, but I couldn't make out the words, no pressure of sound bore the meaning to me. Her face said more, though, it was white, freckled-dusted and sad. I knew what she wanted, what she needed me to do. I looked at her, at myself and spoke, quietly.

"I will do it, Mary, I will try and try to put all this right, let you rest, have your life." She smiled, wanly, and disappeared, like mist burning off in the sun. I sat in Princes Street Gardens, a cardboard coffee carton in my hand, folder open on the table. The sun glazed the beautiful sandstone buildings on the Mound, and the castle sat serenely atop the rock. Everything was the same, but everything was about to change for me. The world shifts on its axis for one person, and no-one else notices. This was the beginning of the end for me, and the ending of the beginning. People on the next bench chatted idly, young mothers with buggies strolled through the gardens and the occasional tourist stopped to click the castle. Everyone going about their daily lives, while I stood on the brink of monumental change. At night, alone in my flat, I laid plans, thought hard, and remembered. As a young journalist in the early 1970s, I remember one of the other reporters snorting with laughter one lunch time as we flicked through the other daily newspapers, while eating chips and drinking Coke. Healthy eating wasn't in vogue then, and we were no doubt about to finish off the meal with a cigarette each."Listen to this!" He flatted out the tabloid on his desk. "Characteristics needed for various occupations... journalist, rat-like cunning required!"

I joined in the laughter at the time: we were well used to slurs upon the profession we'd chosen and knew that collectively, we were seen as almost as untrustworthy as politicians. But maybe cunning was needed for the task ahead of me: cunning and a cool head.

My first task was to track down and talk to Robert Scott. That little boy of decades ago was now an old man, prematurely aged. It took him several minutes to come to the door of his sheltered housing bungalow and let me in. My first thought on seeing him, standing in the doorway, leaning on a stick, was a flicker of doubt that this was the right man. He looked at least 15 years older than he really was: pale, gaunt-featured, and with a worn-out look about him. I sat across from him in the small, overheated sitting room, watching the rise and fall of his chest as he laboured for breath. An oxygen cylinder sat beside his arm chair and his deeply wrinkled face completed the picture of a life-long smoker. He didn't recognise me, of course. As luck, or the social culture of the time would have it, I had changed my surname, both personally and professionally, when Alan and I got married, so there was no danger of recognition.

"It's good of you to see me, Mr Scott," I smiled, clicking on the small recorder I'd laid on the coffee table between us. "As I mentioned in my phone call, I'm researching the history of the police in Edinburgh for an article I'm writing for a magazine. I've got lots of facts and figures, of course, but what I want is the real stories about being a police officer in the nineteen sixties and seventies. You know, what it was really like being on the beat, dealing with trouble, catching the bad lads!" I made my tone light hearted and chatty.

"I'm going to record our conversation and take some notes, to help me write the article. Are you happy with this?"

Sure enough, Robert was only too happy to talk.
He'd left school at 15, and had a few jobs, as a butcher's boy, builder's labourer and then working for a coal merchant, before he was accepted for training as a police cadet. He rose up through the ranks, to become a sergeant, before retiring on health grounds some ten years before.

"Aye, it was good in those days," he mused. "There was plenty of trouble, drugs, house-breakings, car thefts and fights, but somehow, people had a sense of community that they don't have these days. People mostly stayed around where they were brought up. If you were in trouble with the police then everyone knew, so that was a double shame on your head, and on your family, too."

Robert reminisced for two hours, telling me funny and sad stories, chatting, and looking out of the window into the far distance, back into his youth.

"Did you always stay in Portobello?" I asked, casually, writing at the same time.

"Oh no, I've just ended up here in the sheltered housing," he said. "When my health got worse, I moved here. We had a nice house over Newhaven way but it was too big for me once the children grew up and left, and my wife died, of course."

He coughed, a dreadful, racking cough which went on for several minutes. I rose and fetched him a glass of water from the kitchen.

"Thanks," he said, sipping the water. "My lungs aren't up to much, as you'll have gathered. My legs neither," he added, ruefully.

He turned to a black and white photograph in a silver frame on the side table. A large family, gathered for a long-distant celebration. I guessed 1970s from the rigidly formal hairstyles of the women and the shortness of their dresses.

"We had happy times, you know," he said, picking up the photograph and smoothing the frame with his thumb. "I miss her," he added, placing the photograph back on the table

His wife dead, his children dispersed. He was a sad old man, alone with his memories and the black and white ghosts of the past, and struggling with poor health.

The question about where he had lived previously had the desired effect, though. It led him down into the past, and he talked at length about his children: one in Australia, and two in England. Then, almost oblivious to my presence, he began to reminisce about his childhood.

"Aye, our teacher was a real tartar," he said, "but she made sure we all knew our times tables and could spell properly. You got a gie sore hand from the strap if you didn't!" he chuckled.

Nearly there. "Where did you live when you were a lad?" I asked.

Out it came, all the stories of playing football in the street, saving glass lemonade bottles to exchange for entrance to the cinema, or messing about on the building site where they were still throwing up the flats.

I had to make a conscious effort not to hold my breath. Would he buy it?

"You know, I seem to remember something about near where you lived. My cousin went to school with a girl who was put away for killing a wee boy, was it? Throwing a brick at him and killing him dead? Or maybe I'm mistaken..."

I let my voice trail off, unconcerned, while I pretended to study the photos of his twin grandsons, thousands of miles away in Adelaide.

"Lovely children, these," I murmured.

Robert was back where I wanted him to be, on that day in 1958.

"Aye, that was a terrible business, so long ago now, but I'll never forget it," he said. "It was a young girl that was killed, by a half-brick. Jennifer Wilson was her name. She was a wee terror, truth to tell, but it was a shame she died. Her sister Beryl was a bloody evil little bitch, even at the age of ten," he added.

"So what happened?" I asked.

The recorder whirred silently, with its own deadly momentum. Robert seemed to have forgotten it was there. Odd, you'd have thought a former policeman would have paid more attention to what was being recorded. Maybe he'd moved so far from the awareness of his former daily working life that this simply didn't register.

"Well, see there was this girl, Mary McGregor, lived in the flat near us," he began. "She was a stuck up wee madam, thought she was a cut above us because she went to a posh girls school across the town. Her father was a schoolteacher but they didn't have two pennies to rub together. The poor aristocrats, we called them!"

I could feel my hand beginning to shake, a tremor of memory.

Robert continued. "I remember it all fine. Jennifer and Beryl were shouting names at Mary McGregor, over the fence. "Then we started throwing stones as well. Brian Kelly picked up a brick and flung it, but just as he did, Jennifer turned her head and the brick hit her smack on the temple. She died in the hospital later that day."

I struggled so hard to stop my voice from faltering.

"But I thought the girl, what was her name, Mary, did it?"

"Aye, well that was the problem, wasn't it?" he said. "We all knew it was Brian flung the brick but see, he was one of us, and Mary wasn't. We couldn't say it was him. He was almost family. Besides, his father was a real big tough man, a real bad bugger. He would have torn us limb from limb if we'd cliped on Brian."

Robert Scott paused. "We all had to go to the court and give evidence. I was so scared I nearly wet my breeks," he said. "A judge in a black gown telling us to tell the truth, looking over his specs at me from his bench. But we had told the police it was Mary, and we all had to stick to the story. The lassie, Mary, was put away in a reformatory I think, but the family moved away up north soon after that so I don't know what happened."

He looked at me. "I've never been proud of telling that lie, but there really wasn't any choice. I would have been battered from here to kingdom come if I'd told on Brian. In any case," he added," I don't suppose Mary would have been long in the reformatory, a few years at the most. She would have got out while she was still in her teens, I reckon."

Fourteen, actually, I wanted to say, but didn't.

"I wonder what ever happened to Jennifer's family after all that," I said casually. "Did they stay in the same house?"

"Aye, they did," remembered Robert. "They had a lot of relatives nearby, grannies and cousins and the like, a right big family. I believe Beryl's still in the area, although we lost touch years ago. Different paths in life, hen! Beryl was always, well, a difficult lassie, no' the nicest of women, though she was gie upset when Jennifer died."

He shifted a little in his seat, and I saw the wince of arthritis cross his face. Poor man, I thought, life hasn't been kind to you.

"I heard about her not that long ago, as it happens," he continued. "Her man died, her second husband that was, Roy Inglis. My pal Jim was at the funeral at Seafield Crem."

I made a couple of low, encouraging noises.

"Always difficult when these things happen," I ventured. "Was it a while ago?"

He took the bait. "Oh, it was a couple of months ago, July time I think."

I rapidly changed the subject, once more picking up the framed photo of his grandchildren in Australia.

"I can see the family resemblance here, Mr Scott," I said.

"These boys are very like you around the eyes."

He brightened, and smiled.

"Aye, I just wish they were nearer, though. It's a long way for a cuddle!

We talked a little further about the value of Skype, emails and Facebook and I contained my impatience to leave.

I slipped the recorder and my notebook into my bag.

"I hope you're not going to write up all that personal stuff about my family and my childhood, living in the scheme," he said suddenly.

I half-expected this, so was ready with the reply.

"Oh, don't worry about that, Mr Scott," I said, smiling. "I have to gather lots of information when I interview people, but use only some parts of it. For this article, I'm only going to be using the information about your police career when you were a young officer, and some of the wee stories you've told me about your time on the beat. It was very interesting, though, to hear about the games you played as a child, and about your school teachers!"

Keep it all away from the death, take it down a different road, and leave him reassured.

"You'll get to see anything I've written, of course, before it is published," I added.

All of this was in essence true, that was exactly how it worked interviewing someone. People were often disappointed how little of the material they gave me appeared in the finished article.

"But, the tape?" he said. Oh shit. He had come back down to earth and realised that everything he said was on tape.

"Well, what I do is take my notes from the tape, write up the article and then wipe it clean. I've about six or seven interviews on this tape, also with former police officers, and they've told me things 'off the record', naming names about villains and organised crime, drugs barons, pimps and so on." I looked at Robert Scott.

"We have to be incredibly careful about confidentiality and defamation, and of course I have to protect my sources. I'm very scrupulous about note-taking and recording, and apart from wiping, or sometimes destroying tapes, I shred all my paper notes too, after a certain length of time, once the article is published." A gamble now.

"However," I added, "if you aren't comfortable with what you said on tape, I can destroy it right now if you like, and will just rely on my paper notes. You have such a good way of telling the stories, though, I would like to get it right!"

He hesitated, then laughed.

"Oh well, everything is ancient history anyway. I'll just need to trust that you won't land me in any trouble!"

"I'll be in touch soon, Mr Scott. I'll email you a draft piece and you can let me know if you are happy with it."

I took my leave of Robert Scott, glad to be outside in the fresh air again. I waved to him as I closed the gate, and had a final glance of a tall but stooped old man with a bleached, washed-out, set face raise his arm in a final salute to me. I wouldn't ever see him again. I hadn't intended to write up an article, as this had simply been a ruse to get him to talk, but I now felt I had to offer him some reassurance. The last thing I wanted was him making waves.

Once home, I cobbled together an article, using some of his anecdotes and making up some others attributable to fictional retired police officers.

"Dear Mr Scott," I wrote to him a few days later. "Here's the draft article with your comments. Just let me know if you are happy with the wording of your section – sorry it is quite short – and I'll pitch it to a couple of magazines who sometimes take my work. If it ever appears in print I'll send you a copy, but these articles sit on file for many months or even longer. It was nice to meet you, and thanks for sparing the time to see me."

As always, I'd stuck as near to the truth as possible. The lie was that no magazine editor would ever see the article I'd pulled together. That went straight into the dustbin once the letter to Robert Scott had gone off. The only people who would ever hear or read Robert Scott's words would be my children, and then I would do as I had promised him.

The tape would be destroyed.

Chapter Thirteen *Beryl Wilson, and Revelations*

Stick to the truth as near as possible, I kept reminding myself. I was a journalist, so there was no need to fake anything there. Although I was retired from full-time work, I'd kept my NUJ card and retired members' affiliation, so I had identity. I was going to need it for Beryl, and for even more so for my meeting with Brian Kelly. I also needed a second recording device, a miniature one. After the experience with Robert Scott, the near-miss, I wasn't taking any chances of an abortive interview.

Beryl would have been the very devil to find, but for the unwitting evidence of Robert Scott. Twice married, it would have been a difficult task to track her down, even with the modern resources of Google and Facebook.

I made my way back again, to Register House to check the deaths recorded in September and October, then over to the Evening News family announcements archive.

Soon, I had the information needed before I met with Beryl.

"Peacefully, after a long illness bravely borne, on Tuesday 29 July, at St Columba's Hospice, Roy William Inglis, beloved husband of Beryl, father to Kieran, Lauren and Barry, step-dad to Jennifer and Tyrone, and a loving papa to Jay-dee, Aliesha, Jordan, Teighan, and Billy. A dear brother, uncle and friend. Funeral at Seafield Crematorium on Monday 5 October at 11am. Family flowers only but donations to Cancer Research and the Railway Workers Benevolent Fund."

The death notice in the Evening News gave me a huge amount of information, and also a possible opening for my conversation with Beryl, but I carried on with the research, turning next to social media.

 As expected, I was able, very quickly, to get up to speed with the late Roy's family, particularly the younger members.

"We miss you papa, luv u always, Jordan and Teighan."

"Rest peaceful big man"

"We've lost a diamond geezer"

 Beryl, to my slight surprise, also had a Facebook page. I recognised her immediately from her profile picture, she hadn't changed much.

Her face was still hard and set, with the thin, pinched look she had, even as a ten year old.

As a child, she had thick, black hair, dark brown eyes and she was thin and wiry-looking. Her sister Jennifer, and her two brothers, all looked like their father, who was tall with greying red hair and bright blue eyes. Their mother was a harridan, with bleached blonde hair and a shrewish temper.

Looking at the Facebook photo of Beryl, almost 60 years later, the penny finally dropped.

I'd once overheard my parents talking about the Wilson family.

They were in the kitchen, doing the dishes after tea and I was sat at the table in the corner of the livingroom, near to the open kitchen door, ostensibly doing my homework, a page of very hard and very boring sums. Dad had brought me home a pile of coloured scrap paper the day before, and I'd been itching to get going on my latest literary work ever since.

I was planning to write a dramatic play featuring a very brave Brownie, to be played by myself, who saved a child from being bitten by a rabid dog, and who then held a conveniently handy stick between its jaws until the police and the vet arrived. The fact that rabid dogs were unheard of in 1950s Edinburgh did not deter me from setting the play in my home town.

I'd read about mad dogs in a National Geographical magazine in the dentist's waiting room recently and had been filled with a mixture of terror and excitement at the description of the slavering hounds biting and infecting humans. I planned that the rest of the children in the stair would be acting out their parts shortly, as soon as I finished the script. I would, of course, need to persuade the timid Morag to be the rabid dog, suitably draped in an old and moth-eaten fur wrap from my dressing-up box. Now, who to play the policeman, I wondered? Engrossed as I was in the play I was writing, my ears pricked up at the mention by my mother of the name Beryl Wilson.

"Of course, the mother is no better than she should be, you can hardly blame the children for being dirty and smelly, it's up to the adults to make sure they have clean clothes," my mother said as she placed a dripping pot onto the draining rack. "But that Beryl really is an extraordinarily wicked little girl. She seems to delight in causing trouble, she has a sharp tongue and she bullies the younger ones around here, I know. Wee Morag is terrified of her. Her mother told me that just the other day, when we were both queuing in the Post Office."

I kept my head down and listened hard.

"Oh, well, Ruth, the children can't be blamed for the parents' mistakes," said my father, wiping dry the cutlery. "She might turn out alright as she grows up and gets away from her family."

My mother washed the vegetable dish thoughtfully.
"I think there's been a stranger in the camp there, John. Beryl is nothing like the rest of that family. And her mother has been seen at the Bricklayers' Arms in the evenings keeping company with all sorts."

"It would account for much, a cuckoo in the nest and so on," said dad, hanging up the dishtowel.

"Well, we just need to keep our two away from that family as much as possible, until we can get a move out of here," said my mother. "Anything in the Times Ed this week that looks promising?"

I didn't hear dad's reply as he clattered the dishes back up into the cupboard, but shortly afterwards both parents came back into the sitting room and I reluctantly drew my arithmetic book over the yellow pages of my play.

Next day at school, Joyce and I were sitting inside after lunch, which had been particularly tasty that day: shepherd's pie followed by treacle pudding and custard. We were pleasantly full and enjoyed being inside for the break, due to the bleak, driving rain outside. We had our books of scraps with us and had been doing some swapping.

This pleasurable task involved putting all your duplicates from the sheets of scraps bought with your pocket money from the newsagents. The scraps came in shiny, slippery cellophane folders, and hung from a hook near the rack with the crossword puzzle books and writing pads. We each had a large scrap book and into each page was glued a collection of scraps, with different themes. These themes could be animals, fairies, angels, cars, dolls, children in national costume… the list was endless. A doublers book was kept for the duplicates which turned up in the sheets bought at the newsagents, and these were carefully inserted between pages in the book. Doing this kept the scraps in the best condition and retained their swapping value. There was a pecking order with this as with everything else. A large, chubby cherub sitting on a cloud and looking upwards with his chin cupped in his hand could be swapped for two, or even three smaller flower fairy scraps. Unless they were coated in glitter, of course, in which case they had a much higher market value.

We had closed our scrap swap books and were just talking as our lunch was digested. I asked Joyce what it could mean about a stranger in the camp or a cuckoo in the nest.

Joyce, the future lawyer and with a brain like a steel trap, even at the age of eight, pondered for a few moments. She wore glasses even at that age, a situation she deplored but which was to enhance her intellectual look throughout her life. She was to be a woman who always taken seriously.

"Well", Joyce said eventually, "I don't know about the stranger in the camp, unless they went off for a camping holiday and met someone new there and they became friends? Does that sound likely to you?"
"Doesn't sound like them," I replied. "I can't see Mrs Wilson sleeping in a tent, somehow, or cooking on one of those little stoves. She doesn't cook much anyway, Jennifer and Beryl go to the chippie most nights to get everyone's tea, because I've seen them lots of times."

We thought further.
"Do you think it was a camp where people go round the country with their cars pulling those big shiny caravans along, you know, like they have the fair?" I speculated.

Joyce and I had both been taken, at separate times, by our parents to the permanent fair down at Portobello, as a special treat. I had been so excited at the sights and sounds of the helter-skelter and the waltzer, the smell of hot diesel and the crack of air pistols shooting at targets. I was allowed to buy the huge stick of pink candy floss, which I ate too fast and was then sick in the portable toilet next to the fairground.

The romance of hooking up your caravan and moving off to the next town thrilled me to the core, and for weeks afterwards my writing had a distinct Romany flavour. Clothes pegs and lucky heather sold door to door, hedgehog stews cooked over roaring camp fires, and a fortune teller with large hooped gold earrings figured strongly in the plays I wrote for the children in my stair.

Joyce was still mulling over the conversation my parents had had over the washing-up. "Cuckoos don't build their own nests, I do know that," she said. Joyce was very interested in wildlife and cut out articles from magazines and newspapers, which she then glued into a big scrap book with a picture of an owl on the front cover.

"They find a nest that another bird has built and lay their egg in there. Then the baby cuckoo hatches and pushes the other eggs, or the wee fledglings, out of the nest, so it gets all the food," she explained.

She thought further. "I don't see how that would work though, if Mrs Wilson doesn't cook anyway. Maybe Beryl gets more chips that the others.

We looked at each other, knowing there was more to this and not understanding what.

"Well, Beryl is a very horrible person," I confided. "I'm scared of her. Once, she nipped me so hard that I had a big red mark on my arm for days. And she smells, a horrible, fusty smell, her clothes always look dirty. She says things I don't understand, too. About bottoms and boys you-know-whats."

We looked at each other, wondering. We were intelligent, and well-read for our age, but we were still just little girls, at a school where we were sheltered and protected from adult life. Sex was still a firmly closed book, and the remarks Beryl and some of the older children in our stair sometimes made, puzzled me.

"I think my mum really wants dad to get that head of job", I said to Joyce, now bored of the subject of Beryl Wilson and her family. "I hope it's a head of job in Edinburgh so I can stay here at this school. You'll always be my best friend and I don't want ever to leave you."

I'd started reading some of the many books available from the library featuring girls who went to boarding school. My reading age was much above my years, but even so, I was struggling a bit with some of the vocabulary and the social mores. However, I had grasped the idea of deep and meaningful loyalties and friendships amongst the girls, and loved the idea of midnight feasts in the dorms.

My idea of heaven was to have gone to such a school, with Joyce of course, and as far away from my pesky little sister and the horrible Beryl Wilson and her crew as I could possibly be. Joyce was much more down-to -earth than me, and sensibly didn't indulge my fantasies of the future."We don't know what will happen to us. My granny says yesterday is history, tomorrow is a mystery and all we have is the present. I think I understand what she means," said Joyce, "and I don't think she's talking about a birthday present. She means today." Told you she was smart, as well as very literal. Nearly 60 years on from the conversation with Joyce, I looked at Beryl's profile on FaceBook and read her likes section. Some were obvious, Candy Crush, Hibs football team, Gala Bingo and Britain's Got Talent. Some not, though, including one with an acronym, SOCSA, and a logo of a sprig of rosemary, with which I was unfamiliar.

I noted this for later checking, and planned the next move with precision.

After the visit to Curry's to buy a miniature digital recorder, I went home to Google the Railway Workers Benevolent Fund and amass all information I could glean about rail transport in Scotland over the past 40 years or so.

One thing being a journalist taught me was it is always good to have too much information than too little. You can always discard what you don't need. I Googled the unknown website with the rosemary logo, and gasped aloud. Just as well I'd found that out now and not in mid-conversation with Beryl.

I made direct contact with Beryl via a private message on Facebook, asking to meet her to talk about her late husband, for an article on railway workers.
The excuse was a bit flimsier than I would have liked, but I didn't want to go in with the other, bigger thing I'd discovered.

Beryl was obviously intrigued, because she replied a few hours later, giving me her mobile number.

"Hi, Mrs Inglis, thanks for agreeing to meet me," I said, my voice sounding unnatural, hurried, and breathy on the 'phone, despite my best efforts to seem calm. All I could think of as I drove to Beryl's house and parked outside was what she had done to me, what Beryl and Brian had done to me. Somehow, I couldn't bring myself to blame Robert so much.

I paused for a moment before ringing the bell, and collected myself, remembering Aunt Jessie's words. She was right, of course, in what she had said to me. I had lost my childhood, but the Wilsons had lost a child, forever.

Beryl Inglis still lived in the area where we all grew up, only a few streets away from her childhood home in the flats. I now stood on the doorstep of in a pebble dash terraced house with a white uPVC door and two carriage lamps. A bought council house, undoubtedly. As everyone knew, the first thing a tenant turned owner-occupier did was to change the utilitarian front door to one which identified the home's residents as no longer paying rent. The front garden was laid out with red gravel chips, the bleakness broken up by some shrubs and a few garden ornaments: a couple of stone hedgehogs and, yes, two garden gnomes. Their crudely painted faces wore an oddly sinister expression, a fixed grin which didn't match the blankness in their eyes.

"Pull yourself together," said a voice in my head. It might have been my own voice, or perhaps that of the bossy Anne, Aunt Jessie's ghostly colleague from the herbalists. They were both around a lot at the moment and were popping up at inconvenient times.

The front door opened and with immense difficulty, I kept my expression bland. Beryl looked older, of course. Her hair was dyed black, her skin was weathered and bore the tell-tale tiny vertical lines around the mouth, testifying to years of smoking. But she was without doubt the Beryl Wilson I remembered from almost 60 years ago.

Even more disconcerting was her voice.

"Hi, come on it," she said, and I heard her mother's edgy, fractured tone echoing down over the decades. She ushered me into a sitting room which was tidy and well furnished: a three piece leather suite, coffee table, huge television set and a number of china ornaments set along the top of the gas fire surround. "I'll just put the kettle on," said Beryl, and went into the adjoining kitchen.

This gave me valuable minutes to compose myself and look around further.

One entire wall to the left of the chimney breast was filled with family photographs, mostly of children wearing school uniform or sweat shirts with nursery logos. There was a large, gilt-framed photograph in the centre of the collection, showing Beryl as a mature bride with a man who I took to be her recently deceased husband, Roy.

Shelving on the right of the fire held books on railways and gardening, plus some paperback chick lits, and collection of model trains, including a short length of track flanked by a station waiting room, with tiny passengers standing on the platform.

Sipping the coffee I didn't want, I asked her about the models.

"Och, that was Roy. You'd have thought workin' on the railway all they years would have been enough, but he still hankered after the engines even when he retired. Pretended those models were for the bairns visiting, but he widnae let them touch anything!"

She smiled. First time I'd ever seen her do that. As a child, she had a permanent frown on her face. Funny that I'd never noticed that about her.

We chatted, I admired her wall of family photos and her ornaments, and then brought out the recorder with which I'd interviewed Robert Scott.

Stick to the truth, as much as possible, and start with the truth, my inner voice reminded me.

"I'm a semi-retired journalist who writes mostly for magazines nowadays", I said, showing her my NUJ card.

"I'm gathering up some information on men and particularly their families who worked on the railways, and saw an obituary notice a few months ago for your husband, showing his connection to the railways." I paused. Partly true, but a bit flimsy. I smiled apologetically at Beryl.

"Unfortunately the obituaries columns are often the places to find the families of retired men who worked on the railways and who have passed away. I'm doing the same for former mine-workers and their families." Half true.

"I'm interested to know what it was like for the wives and children of the railway employees. Was it hard that they were on shift work and did you get some nice train trips as a wee bonus?"

Beryl lit a cigarette.

"Well, see, Roy was my second husband and he was workin'
on the railways when I met him. He was daft on trains, like a
bairn. It wasn't like a job tae him, it was like a hobby, an' he
got paid!" She laughed.

Dear Lord. I'd never heard her laugh either. Not one single
time when we were children had I ever heard Beryl laugh.

Beryl told me about her life with Roy, his job with the railway
and how the family benefitted from his travel concessions.

"We had a few nice days off to Largs and up to Stonehaven,
and down tae Newcastle and such like."

She seemed relaxed and at ease, so I then drew her into other
areas.

"You must miss him a lot," I said.

She lit another cigarette.

"Aye, well, ma first man wasn't up tae much. Battered me
and the bairns and spend most o' his pay in the pub before it
ever reached me. He was ok when he was sober but he just
changed into a right nutter when he got a drink on him," she
said, quite matter-of-factly.

Crumbs. I wouldn't have thought Beryl would have put up
with a burst pay packet coming in the door. Just goes to show,
people change.

"So Ah left him went back tae ma mother's hoose wi' the bairns, then we were overcrowded wi' all o' us and mother too, so Ah got ma ain flat", she continued. "Ah was workin' nights at the pub along the road – ma mother babysat the bairns – where Roy was a regular. His marriage had broken up tae, and he used tae blether a lot with me. He wisnae a big drinker, though, Ah liked that about him after all the trouble in the first marriage. Then one night he asked me tae go out wi' him on a proper date, like, dinner and everything."

She smiled at the memory. "Naebody had ever been nice tae me like that. We had a richt fancy dinner, yin o' they Italian places up Leith Walk. Wine an' a', and a silly violinist playing. I kent it wisnae Roy's usual thing either: he left the waiter a massive tip, far o'er much. Ah had tae stop masel' saying anything in case it hurt his feelings.
"That wis the start o' it. He wis a good man, treated me an' the bairns right, an, well, then I got pregnant wi' Keiran. That's when he asked me to marry him."

She paused. "We'd been watchin' Casualty and eatin' a fish supper and pickled onions – Ah coudnae get enough of then when Ah wis carrying Keiran – when he suddenly said he thought we should get married afore the bairn arrived."

She smiled again. "No awfy romantic, like, but, he wis a good man. Yes, I miss him, a' the time."

Her face softened, and then looked sad.

"He had a bad deal there, dying o' cancer only four years after he retired. He made me happy, made me feel safe."

I looked over at her. "Sounds like you were lucky with him, though. Have you still got family round here? You mentioned staying with your mother, so I guess your parents must be nearby."

She drew on her cigarette and blew out a stream of smoke.

"Ma da died a long time ago, when Ah wis a teenager" she said, looking at the gas fire. "Ma mother is in a home, she's got that dementia. I go and see her, but she disnae ken me, no' really. She wis startin' tae wander a bit when Roy and I had only been married a couple of years, but she managed ok for quite a while.

"It was just gradual for a long time, and of course being a stubborn woman she wouldnae go near a doctor. But then she jist went richt doon hill the last two years and there wisnae any choice but for her tae go intae a hame."

She paused. "Ma twae brithers live in Edinburgh wi' their families, one's at Granton and the other one stays jist up the road. Ah had a sister too, but she died when she wis seven."

"She died?" I said, feeling in my jacket pocket for a tissue and switching on the miniature recorder. "How dreadful for you to lose your sister so young. Was she ill for long?"
Beryl, just like Robert Scott had done, seemed to be wandering into the past.
"Naw, it wisnae that. Are you still recording?" she asked suddenly.
"Oh, goodness, I'm so sorry," I said, making a show of stopping and switching off the recorder on the coffee table, and putting it away in my brief case.

Beryl gave a half smile and continued.
"Well, we were playing outside in the back green yin day and there wis a bit o' trouble wi' the lassie in the next stair. She was alright really, but she went to a different school across the toon and we kinda picked on her.
"She wisnae doin' anything really, just lying on the shed roof, but well, me an' ma' sister started tae ca' her names and then we were chucking stanes at her."
I murmured that children could be cruel to each other.

"Aye," said Beryl. "Then one of the laddies chucked this big brick o'er the fence at her but it bashed ma sister bang on the side o' her heid. She wis taken tae the Infirmary, but she died a few hours later.

"The doctor said it was just the way the brick hit her, an inch here or there and she might have been alright. But we'll never know."

"How terrible for you," I said. "And the boy who threw the brick must have felt awful. What happened?"

God, I could get into RADA with this performance.

Beryl lit yet another cigarette. She'll be joining the late Roy at the pearly gates at this rate, I thought. If she doesn't have a heart attack, lung cancer's on the cards.

"Well, that's the awfae thing," said Beryl. "We a' lied to the polis and said the wee lassie, Mary wis her name, Mary McGregor, had done it. We didnae want tae let on who it wis, a laddie caud Brian, because Mary wisnae like us, and Brian wis.

"He wis frae a right rough family, his da wis a brute and we were a' feart o' him, but they were the same as us."

"Would your own mother and father not have protected you from Brian's father, if you had spoken the truth?" I asked, my heart racing and mouth dry. Please, oh please let this work.

"Ye dinnae understand," said Beryl, looking at me intently. "Ma family wisnae much better. Ma mother wis too keen on goin' oot and havin' a good time wi' other blokes tae bother aboot us."

She paused again. "Ah didnae find oot until a lot later that ma da wisnae really ma da. Mother had had a fling wi' some travelling salesman she met down the pub and got pregnant wi' me.

"They guessed richt away when I wis born, seemingly, I wasnae ma da's bairn, I didnae look anything like him or ma sister and brothers. But in thay days there wis often bairns lik' that, folk jist didnae talk aboot it or make the palaver they wid today. Everyone jist carried on as if Ah was ma da's bairn."

"How did you find out he wasn't your dad?" I asked.

"Well, it wis a funny thing, "she said. "When I wis aboot 14, Ah had a bad accident on the way hame from school. Ah wis muckin' aboot wi' ma pals and yin o' them dared me to walk alang this high-up auld wall. Well, Ah got up there ok but it had been raining and ma foot slipped on the wet moss on the top an' Ah fell ten feet ontae a pile o' bricks.

"Ah very near died," she said. "Ah had a broken leg and arm, cracked ribs, concussion and a ruptured spleen. I was ok once they operated but Ah'd lost a lot o' blood an' they checked ma and dad's blood groups as well as mine when they were getting blood over frae the transfusion centre. Ah heard a' the talk aboot it, lyin' on the trolley wi' ma eyes closed. Ah heard the doctor telling ma mother that they'd sent a taxi to the blood transfusion place to pick up the supplies before they took me to the operating theatre to tak' ma spleen oot."

She smiled ruefully. "Ah wisnae daft, ye ken. One day after the operation, I wis dozin' and heard the doctor talkin' quiet behind the curtain tae ma mother. He said: 'Mrs Wilson, there's something of an issue with Beryl's blood group. It's quite a rare one, and you – and your daughter too, when she's older – need to know about this should anything happy in the future and she needs a blood transfusion again."

"I heard him clear his throat an' shuffle his feet a bit. Then he said: 'Beryl's blood type is incompatible with your husband being her biological father. This is delicate, Mrs Wilson, but, is Beryl the offspring of a previous, er, marriage?'"

"Ma mother's reply was priceless," said Beryl. "She said to the doctor: 'Doctor, Beryl is the offspring of a previous, er, fling wi' a bloke whit scarpered pronto when he kent he'd knocked me up. Me an' ma lawful wedded husband have brought the bairn up in oor family and there is nae need for ma man tae hear any o' this aboot blood groups and delicate matters and such like. It's ma business, doctor, an' Ah'll thank you to keep that information strictly tae yirself.'"
Beryl laughed at the memory, although it can't have been great hearing that from behind the hospital curtains.

"Your mother sounds very feisty," I ventured, thinking of the woman I'd known, the battle axe, the selfish harridan who had finally succumbed to dementia. Well, she won't remember any of this now, I thought. Her rich and colourful past wasn't even a memory for her.

"Aye, she wis. A richt tartar, naebody could mess wi' her," smiled Beryl.

Beryl looked at me for the first time in many minutes, then said slowly:

"He wis abusing me, ma da, an' Ah didnae ken whit tae dae. There wis naebody tae tell, naebody. He said he wid get me ta'en away to a home for bad girls if Ah ever telt anyone, because everyone wid say Ah wis a dirty wee liar and a troublemaker. "Ma mother wouldnae hae believed me, an' even if she had, she widnae hae pit him oot. He wis the breadwinner, see, and women like ma mother, for a' her carryings-on, wid hae been lost withoot her man. Things were different then."People didnae speak aboot things the way they dae noo. Kids weren't believed anyway. Look at a' they puir wee bairns that were abused by priests and sic like, naebody believed them either, it's a' jist comin' oot noo. In they days, there wis nae rape crisis centres, nae Women's Aid, nae Childline. See, Ah wasnae his bairn so in his twisted head it wis ok tae abuse a ten year old wee lassie.

"Ah've dealt wi' it a' noo," she said, flatly. "Ah had a wee breakdoon after ma last bairn wis born, Ah had that post-natal depression but somehow it a' came oot then when Ah wis at the doctors aboot that. The doctor pit me in touch wi' this group ca'd Survivors of Childhood Sexual Abuse. They've helped me a lot, an' Ah ken fine it wisnae ma fault, Ah wis just a wee lassie. It was a' him, the black bastard!"

Rosemary for remembrance. The logo of SOCSA.

As if she read my mind, she said: "Oor symbol is rosemary, for remembrance. Means we never forget whit happened, but there's a place for it noo. It's like it's in a wee box, an' A've turnt the key, lockin' it awa'. Only Ah can open that box an' look inside, Ah've got the power and the control."

I said nothing, and kept my face impassive. Beryl was clearly quoting from SOCSA literature, but if it helped her to live her life, then who was I to criticise?

Suddenly, I wished that I could compartmentalise all the bits of my life, past and present, and unlock the various boxes at will. It wasn't like that though, all fairly random, and much of it out of my control.

Beryl had found a way to control her life. I hadn't, hence my micro-management of the things I had been able control in life with Alan. There had been a pattern to our lives, dictated by me, I recognised.

We did the big Tesco shopping on Friday nights after work; I changed all the bedding on Saturdays and he cut the grass on Sundays.

No wonder I drove him into the arms of another woman. He must have felt like a robot being programmed to function in a certain way, and to order. I'm sorry, Alan, I thought, not for the first time.

I pulled myself back from my own epiphany moment and listened to Beryl as she spoke further of the man she'd called dad, but who wasn't.

"When he died, Ah felt like someone had lifted a black shadow off of me," said Beryl. "Ah wanted tae dance on the lid o' his coffin. Ah've often wondered if Ah wid have had the courage to shop him to the polis when Ah wis grown up, but he wis lang deid by then."

Beryl was still talking, which didn't surprise me at all. In my experience, once a person has the ear of a sympathetic stranger, who knows no-one connected to them, they will talk for Scotland. It's a safe outlet, and I've never minded listening to anyone.

"Ah've aye felt bad aboot that, blaming the wee lassie when it was really Brian," Beryl went on, returning to the subject of her late sister's death.

"Mary got sent to some kinda approved school and her family moved away, some place up north, I think it was.

"Ah wis a bad wee bitch in those days, Ah should hae' spoken up an' telt the truth, but Ah kent it was partly ma' fault for shoutin' an' callin' her names, and egging on the laddies tae chuck stanes. Ah kent Ah'd be in big trouble as well as Brian, so Ah jist stuck tae the story we'd a' made up. Ma wis jist beside hersel' when Jennifer died, an' ma da just collapsed wi' grief. He had tae leave the funeral service, he wis greetin' that much.

"Ah really felt sae jealous o' Mary, she seemed tae hae a nice family, an' a nice wee sister tae."

Oh Sandra. I'm sending you a huge bunch of flowers once all this is over. I never appreciated what a nice wee sister I had.

We sat for a few moments in silence.

"I'm sure everything worked out for the little girl," I said, untruthfully. "It is all so long ago now, I expect everyone has forgotten all about it."

I looked across the room again, at the wall of photos.

"You have a lovely family, and you've come through so much," I said. "You just need to let things rest, back in the past, where they belong, and look forward to seeing your grandchildren and great grandchildren grow up."

I rose, and added: "I'll let you know if I use any of the information about railway life which you've been kind enough to share with me."

To my surprise, she stretched out her hand to shake mine.

"Yir an awfae gid listener!" she smiled.

My legs were shaking so much that I only drove half a mile from Beryl's house and found a space to park in a quiet side street. I took out a large road map and spread it over the steering wheel, for the benefit of any casual passers-by, while I wept silently onto the open pages, my tears creating huge, wet blotches on the city bypass and trickling right down the map as far as Penicuik.

When I'd recovered myself, I drove the few streets to the block of flats where I'd lived, all those years ago.

I parked nearby, but not outside, my old home, and walked casually along the street, turning into the path which led to the close door.

I noticed that the front gardens had improved from the scrubby wasteland of my childhood. Areas of well-tended grass were bordered by flower beds, and there were mature shrubs lending colour to the entrance to the flats.

The main door was standing wide open, which I took as a sign to carry on. If challenged, I'd just apologise and say I'd got the wrong block of flats.

The hallway of the stair, the scene of enactment of many of my dramatic plays, was freshly painted and the floor had a rubberised covering, not the hard, cold stone I remembered. I walked the few steps along the passageway to the back door and out into the back green. Everything was exactly as I remembered it – the bucket shed, the drying green beyond with its painted iron poles and plastic-coated washing lines strung between them.

Some towels and sheets flapped in the breeze, no longer in danger of being spoiled by smuts of ash. In Edinburgh, as elsewhere, there were no coal fires blazing in beige-coloured grates and so no thick pall of smoke hanging constantly over the housing estate throughout the winter months.

The only real difference in the back green was that in place of the chain-link wire fencing running between concrete posts to separate the adjoining block's back green, a thick, high privet hedge grew, screening the greens from each other.

"Everything is so much smaller, the bucket shed lower, the back green shorter," I thought, then shook myself mentally. Of course it seemed smaller, I had been a little child.

I was walking slowly back along the hallway towards the open door when I felt the hand slipping into mine, light and small, delicate, warm. The little girl, dressed in her 1950s school uniform, leather satchel on her back, and with a dark blue ribbon holding back her mass of red curls, looked up at me and smiled.

I knelt down right there in the hallway and hugged the child I had been, the child who made me what I am today, the child I will always cherish and for whom I will right this wrong. The child who has saved me.

I felt the roughness of her school blazer, and caught the faint mingling of the scents of the child: Pears soap, washing powder, the smell of a sugary sweetie, the acrid sandalwood smell of a sharpened pencil leaching from her schoolbag.

She put her arms around my neck, and I held her tightly, just for a few seconds, before she disappeared with a tiny sigh and a faint, final tug at my sleeve.

I made my way out of the close. Attuned to decades ago now, my nostrils picked up the waft of tar, molten where the men laid the pavements here 60 years ago, and the smell of chips frying in the long-ago closed fish bar. I heard the ragman's hooter sound, announcing his arrival in the street, and saw his pony standing patiently, hooked to an open cart. The cars in the street disappeared as everything faded back to an earlier scene, where I watched the ragman give children balloons and a few pennies for the bags of rags their mothers had collected.

Glancing in the other direction, I saw the children playing on the forbidden building site, clambering around the foundation bricks of the next block of flats. The newness was raw, scarring the muddy earth.

I glimpsed Brian Kelly hitting another boy as my friend Morag watched from a safe distance, clutching her woollen-clad doll. I saw Gummy George jumping over the piles of bricks, the lesson of his accident still to come.

And I saw the last glimpse of myself, on the edge of the tableau, observing, alone, set apart by my different school uniform.

It was all there, my childhood before the death, and just as swiftly gone again. The quiet street was deserted, a radio could be heard playing faintly from an upper window and in the distance, there was the muffled thrum of traffic from the main road.

I got back into the car, and drove away.

Predictably, I cried some more that night, alone in my flat, but this time, the tears were for the beginning of the ending, the settling, not of regret and sorrow.

Chapter Fourteen *Finding Brian Kelly*

I parked the car in a side street in Newington, and stepped onto the pavement, carefully avoiding the protruding roots of the ancient trees which burst through the tarmac.

The shop was easy to find, I'd done all the checking before I left the house. It was a small, glass-fronted shop, set between a delicatessen and a coffee shop, both of which were busy, I noted. This was student land, wealthy student-land at that.

Brian Kelly's shop window glinted in the cold sunshine. I glanced at the display of laptops and sleek retro radios, set on chrome plinths. No prices on show. Classy.

Pushing open the door, there was no uncouth jangle of a bell to alert the staff. They were ready for the customers.

The shop was larger than it appeared from the slim window front. Browsing amongst the hifis and headphones, I spotted the partly–open door into a workshop.

A faint whiff of soldering irons and heat from televisions emanated, and there was muffled music. Radio 2, accompanying the technicians as they repaired, restored and renovated.

"Is this a good one?" I picked up one of the retro look radios, made to look like a 1950s wireless set, but slim, sleek and finished in mint green. I was half-minded to buy it, it looked so appealingly nostalgic as it sat, serene and untroubled by change.

"Oh yes, we sell lots of these," the young shop assistant replied. He fetched over the brochure. "Great tone, very reliable, last you years," he said.

The boy smelled faintly of shampoo and fabric conditioner. Still lives at home, mum does his washing, I guessed. "It's lovely, does it get all the digital channels?" I enquired.

He continued the sales pitch, I asked the right questions, then said: "This shop's been here a long time, hasn't it?"

The boy was thrown for the first time in our conversation. "I dunno, really. This is a Saturday job for me, I'm still at school and I only started here last year."

An older woman sitting at a corner counter, next to a cash register, looked up from her paperwork.

"Oh, this shop's been here since 1975. It was the first one Mr Kelly opened. Had a few upgrades and repaints since then, of course!" She smiled, and fingered the double strand of pearls at her neck.

"I was just a youngster like Adam here when the shop opened. It was my first and last job: you could say I grew with the company."

 I smiled back, taking in the heavily made-up face and immaculately-permed grey hair large-lensed spectacles magnifying her brown eyes.
"Gosh, that's interesting!" I had genuine enthusiasm in my voice. I'd hit pay dirt, and so fast!

 The woman settled for a chat, looking not at me, but into the mid-distance, not seeing the crowded pavement, the pigeon swooping on crumbs, or the first cloud gathering across the sun. Adam turned away, thwarted, and put back the radio brochure in a drawer.

"Yes, I'd just turned 16 and I was taken on as a clerical assistant. Mr Kelly was young himself then, just getting established."

She smiled, remembering. "He needed someone to do the paperwork, and make up the wages on a Friday. Little brown pay packets in those days, and everyone paid in cash!
"I remember his words clearly. He said: 'If you work hard, you'll do well here, Doreen. The sky's the limit!'"

I kept smiling and spoke quietly. "You must have been his right-hand woman," I coaxed.

Doreen gave a self-deprecating half-smile.
"Oh yes. He says he can't do without me. Of course, I'm in charge of the administration and salaries for all the shops these days, as well as for the small workshop here, and the main workshops in Leith," she said, triumphantly.
"Fancy that," I said, wondering how to keep this thread of conversation going, praying her phone wouldn't ring. I needn't have worried. Doreen was well underway on her trip into the past.
"Let's see now," she mused, gazing out through the window. "He opened this shop in 1975, just him, me, an engineer and a girl to man the desk and the till while I did the paperwork. All those orders for spare parts and new equipment, not to mention sending out accounts, booking in the van for servicing, keeping the bills paid, such a lot of work!"

She loved every minute of it, that was clear, but there was something else, just eluding me…

"Mr Kelly was Ferranti-trained you know." Doreen looked at me, making sure I realised the importance of this remark. Ferranti had been a big presence in the new world of television manufacture in Edinburgh in the 1950s. "He went there straight from school and never looked back," she added, smiling proudly. "Of course, he went to night school after a day's work to learn all the technicalities. None of this full-time college that they have these days!"

So that's what happened to him then. I could the stiffness settling across my face as my smile fixed hard. "Yes, Mr Kelly worked day and night to build the business," Doreen smiled." He would be out fixing tvs and radios – fairy lights and irons too – day and night, weekends too. What a worker!"

Doreen gazed out of the window and back in time into Edinburgh of the 1970s.

"Then he opened the other shops, in the New Town, up Gorgie way and eventually out of the city into Midlothian," she remembered.

"Didn't his wife mind him working all these hours?" I asked, smiling.

Doreen stiffened slightly and her smile dropped a millimetre or so.

"Oh, Mrs Kelly was taken up with looking after their girls. She left all the business side of things to him. And to me, of course!" She trilled, in a quite contrived, self-effacing manner, inviting contradiction.

Of course. Doreen and Brian Kelly had been lovers. There would have been late nights working together, when she was doing the books or stocktaking and he was in the workshop soldering dry joints.

I pictured them sharing a takeaway from the chippie and a couple of bottles of beer after a long evening's work, chatting, flirting. Doreen, in awe of her hard-working boss, and Brian Kelly, flattered by Doreen's attentions and her firm, untrammelled flesh, her dolly-bird clothes.

Mrs Kelly, back home, exhausted by two babies under three, would have sunk into bed and been snoring gently when Brian got home. Doreen was willing, there was no harm done.

But there had been harm done. I knew it with such utter certainty that Doreen might just as well have told me straight out.

I noted her ringless left hand, and pictured her neat, soulless flat, the M&S meal for one in the fridge, then the empty, endless space of a lonely evening.

A solitary retirement was looming for her, as was the spectre, ever-present, of a Christmas alone, an unnoticed tree, a mini-trifle for one, the Queen's speech, followed by a few sherries too many, and silent tears shed as she remembered the past and thought sadly of what might have been

I knew that this was my last chance here, my last throw of the dice, before she began to suspect, or before she's drawn back to her work.

"I expect it was all worth it though, for Mr Kelly," I ventured, pretending to examine a silver coffee making machine which looked far too complicated to use. "I bet he doesn't have to fix tvs nowadays."

Doreen smiled again. "It's mostly computers and hi-fis we do nowadays, but no, Mr Kelly doesn't repair things himself these days. He's semi-retired in any case. Matthew, his wife's nephew, is general manager."

"He must be finding other things to do," I said.

"Well, he plays a lot of golf and sees the grandchildren," Doreen said. There was the tiniest frost in the air. "He has a lovely big villa up in Morningside, and they entertain a lot. I've been to their house quite a few times, helping out, you know." Her eyes brightened again.

Bingo! I couldn't believe how easy this was turning out to be, and it was so lucky that the three people I was seeking had all remained in their home city. So Brian Kelly has a villa in Morningside, and is a member of a golf club. He shouldn't be too hard to find.

Don't tell any lies if you can help it, and stick to the facts where possible, admit you met Doreen, keep it as simple as possible, I kept reminding myself as I punched in Brian Kelly's phone number. "Hello, Mr Kelly? My name is Mary Millar and I'm a freelance journalist. I write for the Scotsman and Evening News sometimes…. Oh, you know my name! I mostly write for magazines these days," I said, keeping my voice friendly and light.
"Well, I happened to be in your Newington shop the other day and got chatting to a lady there, Doris was it? Sorry, no, it was Doreen… she mentioned how you'd built up the business from a small start in the 1970s. Yes, time flies, doesn't it?"

Keep calm. He mustn't get the slightest hint.

"I'm writing a feature for a Scottish business magazine about self-made men and women who have built up businesses, created jobs and so on. I think you fit ideally into this category, and I'd love to chat to you," I continued, keeping my voice steady.

"Yes, Thursday at eleven at your house? That would be ideal. Look forward to seeing you then."

My hands trembled as I put down the sweat slicked phone. Looking in the mirror, I saw I had actual beads of sweat on my brow. This can't happen on Thursday....

Chapter Fifteen *First Visit to Brian Kelly*

 With an irony not lost to me, Brian Kelly lived in a villa very near to the house where Morningside Mary lived in the 19th century.

His home was a lovely sandstone house, set on a rise from the tree-lined street, with fine bay windows overlooking a terraced, well –tended front garden laid mostly to shrubs. The sturdy front door with it brass lion's head knocker looked to be the original fitment.

Brian Kelly opened the door, and, as at my encounter with Beryl Wilson, I recognised him instantly.

A wash of fear ran through me, hoping he hadn't had a similar *frisson* of familiarity when he saw me. But I already knew that I would be seeing him, and he was expecting to see an unknown journalist. So that's all that he saw. He led me along a wide hallway into the elegant lounge.

At a glance, I could see that Brian was extremely affluent and had spent a lot of money on his home. Every fitment and item of furniture was exquisitely perfect and in keeping with the age of the house. The paintings decorating the walls were few but tasteful – l spotted a John Bellany and an Elizabeth Blackadder – and the wallpaper and curtains were clearly from an expensive, bespoke city outlet.

The boy from the scheme had made good.

Brian himself had borne the passage of time well. In stark contrast to my encounter with Robert Scott, this time I sat across from a well-toned, fine-looking man, with grey hair, certainly, but with a tanned, handsome face. His clothes were casual but of good quality. He reeked of money.

He brought through coffee on a tray and we chatted about the weather, gardening and the city's trams project before I began the interview in earnest.

Once more, I stuck as near to the truth as possible, showing my credentials, explaining I was a semi-retired freelance journalist who mostly wrote for magazines.

"As I explained, Mr Kelly, I'm looking for a few examples of city businessmen who are what you might call 'self-made'. I understand that you built your business up from quite small beginnings?"

He smiled, and told me his story, which was in essence the same as the narrative with which Doreen had regaled me in the shop that day.

Brian Kelly was interested in my recording machine, which, as with Robert and Beryl, I placed on the coffee table.

"I could get you a much more up-to-date version of this," he said, examining the machine. "More compact, better tone. If you want to pop into one of my shops some time and mention my name, they'll give you it trade price." He smiled, showing immaculate teeth.

Capped, I thought. I asked him about his early working life, and how he started out in business for himself.
He told me virtually what Doreen had done about his training with Ferranti and his efforts to establish his first business. He let slip one piece of information though, which I tucked away for future use.

"Yes, I worked all the hours God sent," he remembered, his hands resting on the arms of his leather armchair. "I really wanted the business to succeed, and knew there was no room for slacking off. My father-in-law, Tony, lent me the money to get started, to rent the shop, buy a van and tools and so on." He looked over at me, saying quickly: "I paid him back, of course, once I really started to pull in the money, but I'll never forget how he helped me at the beginning."

"You must have been very grateful, and I'm sure he's proud of all you've done since," I murmured.

"Well, Tony was a self- made businessman himself, and had a couple of garages when I first knew him. He'd used his army training as a motor engineer, and his Forces gratuity and pension, to set up on his own after the war," he explained.

Then Brian Kelly smiled.

"That's how I met my wife, Marie, actually. I took my very old and very unreliable car to Tony's garage one day and she was in the office, doing the paperwork. We got chatting and I discovered she went to the same church as me, St Martin's."

Well, blow me down! I knew that Brian's family was Roman Catholic, but somehow I didn't imagine him attending church as an adult, which just goes to show that you shouldn't ever jump to conclusions.

Brian, oblivious to my inner surprise, continued with his story. "Well, I saw Marie soon afterwards at a church social – can't think why I hadn't seen her before, she was stunningly good looking – and I asked her out on a date. We courted for a while, became engaged and then we married."

"What family do you have?" I asked.

"Two girls", he said. "One was an air hostess and she married a pilot. They live up at the Braids now. My other daughter is an accountant and she's a partner with a firm in East Lothian, where she lives. She's married to a police inspector. I've five grandchildren now," he added, smiling, his eyes softening. "Two boys and three girls. The boys are wee terrors. We put away all the ornaments when those laddies visit!"

The bile rose in my throat and right at that moment, I wanted to leap from my chair and strangle him, as he sat there, smugly.

You ruined my life, you bastard, I thought, and you sit there talking about your successful family and your lovely grandchildren

"Keep calm," said the voice in my head. Aunt Jessie this time, I think.

I fished in my pocket for a tissue and switched on the miniature tape, just as I'd done at Beryl's, and led Brian back to his childhood. He made no secret of where he'd been brought up, although he made little reference to his family, simply saying that both his parents were dead and he didn't have much to do with his brothers and sisters.

"We weren't a close family, really. I have my own family now," he said, a little stiffly.

Well, I thought, that's a nice neat sentence to obliterate all memory of that gang of rogues from which he sprang.

Like Robert and Beryl, he remembered playing on the building site, the horse-drawn ragman's cart, the games of football on the scrubland and his sisters playing peevers in the street with an old polish tin acting as a counter on the chalk-drawn flags.

"I seem to remember there was a child died down your way, killed by another child?" I said, appearing to remember with difficulty. "My cousin went to the same school as the killer, there was quite a scandal at the time, I remember."

The tension was palpable Brian Kelly shifted in his chair and his face took on a blankness. Only the movement of his fingers clenching and unclenching showed his inner disquietude. Then he spoke. "Yes, I saw it happen, I'll never forget it. Mary, the girl who did it, was a stuck-up wee madam, with plenty of airs and graces about her. She used big words a lot, and even if we didn't know what they meant, we knew she was being nasty. She went to a private school across the town, and she didn't think much of us local kids."

He paused. "Her father was only a schoolteacher, too. Nothing special."

With a huge effort, I kept my fixed smile in place, and murmured a few platitudes, lies of course, about teaching being an easy number. Sorry dad, sorry Alan, and sorry all my teacher friends who work so hard. I had to keep Kelly on side. Brian Kelly tented his fingers and continued:"There was a lot of name calling one day when we were out in our back greens. Me and my pal Robert were kicking around a football when we heard Mary saying some nasty things to the girls, two sisters, Jennifer and Beryl Wilson."

You lying piece of shit, I screamed inwardly.

He carried on with his story. "Then this Mary got really angry and started shouting and screaming at Jennifer. She picked up a half brick and flung it right at her, straight over the fence. It hit Jennifer hard on the temple, and she went bang straight down on the ground. She died that afternoon in the hospital, a massive brain haemorrhage."

He looked at me. "Bad luck in some ways, maybe, just the way and place the brick hit Jennifer. An inch or so of difference and she might have lived. I don't suppose Mary intended to kill her, but she wanted to harm her, that's for sure. She had a nasty temper on her, that girl. Jennifer's family were devastated, of course. There was a trial where we all had to give evidence, and Mary was sent away to an approved school somewhere up north, I believe." He added: "I expect she was only there a couple of years, though."

Why does everyone think that? I wondered. First Robert Scott, now Brian Kelly. Once more, I wanted to say, it was six years of my life. I was there for murder, remember, Jennifer died, and you all told the sheriff that I meant to harm her. It wasn't seen as an accident in the eyes of the law. It was seen as a deliberate act.

I collected my thoughts, switched off the tape, shook Brian Kelly's hand, resisting the temptation to squeeze his bones till they cracked. I took my leave, promising to return to show him a draft article and also to collect old photographs from him, of his first workshop, which he promised to look out for me.

I had failed. He hadn't confessed, instead he'd lied, and perpetuated the lie of almost 60 years ago. I had the testimony of Robert Scott and Beryl Wilson to prove my innocence, but I needed Brian Kelly to confess, on tape. This whole thing had to be absolutely watertight if my family was to be convinced of the injustice done to me.

I drove home in silence, my mind racing.

Chapter Sixteen *Saving Jamie*

I needed to focus, to think, to clear away the mists, to find a way to get Steven back there, to save Jamie from drowning, and to put things right for High Street Mary. The trouble was, although I was very used to both Marys, not to mention other long-dead relatives, bobbing in and out of my life, sometimes at very inconvenient moments, I hadn't ever tried to conjure them up at will. They all had minds of their own, and chose when to appear, or not.

Then there was the problem of involving Steven in this endeavour. He'd need to be told, to overcome his natural scepticism and to co-operate with my plan.

"Not been in here for a long time, not since my student days. Always liked it though, great atmosphere."

My son sat back on the oak settle and looked around at the dark panelled walls of the low-ceiling pub in the High Street. They were hung with 18th century prints and brass bellows, for the enjoyment of tourists. The pub was as near a location as I could get to where Mary had lived in the 18th century. Proximity might be helpful, I had reasoned.

Steven took a swig from his pint glass, while I sipped at a gin and tonic. He looked at me, hardening his gaze.

"I'm not taking any more letters to Phoebe, mum. She and Cam are settled, and she's not wanting any contact with you, or upset, especially now that..." His voice tailed off and I saw the same furtive look he had as a small boy when he'd broken something or teased his sister.

Pregnant. Phoebe was pregnant. He didn't even need to tell me, I knew.

"It's about Phoebe, and you, and other things, Steven," I began.

I saw him shuffle, uncomfortable.

"Mum, this is difficult for me. You know that I try hard not to take sides..."

"Yes, I know, Steven. It has been dreadful for you, and I'm so sorry." I held my son's gaze. "I have to tell you some things, and I want you just to listen, and not be alarmed. I'm not crazy, deluded or possessed.

"You don't need to worry about me, or yourself. I want to tell you how things are, and how they've been."

In a quiet, measured tone, I told Steven about having lived before, twice, in Edinburgh. I described High Street Mary, and the death by drowning of her small brother, Jamie. I told him about Morningside Mary, Elizabeth, Walter and the letter I burned in 1854, and the disastrous consequences. Then, I brought him up to date with my efforts to prove my innocence over the Jennifer Wilson killing.

He sat, listening carefully, with the occasional glance at me, and the odd stifled gasp.

When I finished, he took a long pull on his pint, then looked at me.

"I believe you, mum. None of this is a surprise to me."

"What!" I exclaimed. That wasn't quite the reaction I expected.

"Of course I believe you," he said. "I see things all the time which are from the past. People flit in and out of my life too, who couldn't and shouldn't be there. It's always been like this for me: the ghost in our flat in the Old Town, old horse-drawn carriages in the High Street, Victorian ladies walking through doors and ragged beggars from the middle ages. I see carts pulled through the streets, and sometimes there are bare-footed children tugging at my jacket."

He paused. "My office is in an old building, as you know, and it can get quite crowded in there with people past and present!" He laughed, but there was an edge to his words.

"And I saw a unicorn on The Meadows the other evening, when I was out jogging with my mate Joe from work. I thought it was a white pony at first, but then I saw the horn!"

I sat in silence for a few moments, my head whirling, before I spoke again.
I smiled across at my son.
"Well, I'm glad it isn't just me who sees all these things which shouldn't be there."
He smiled back, a knowing grin.

For the next few minutes, I sat in silence, thinking over what my son had just revealed.

You see, because the Marys, and other long-dead relatives have a habit of popping up into my life from time to time, they pull other things along with them, out of the past, out of the rich soup of myth, legend, folklore, truths and half-truths, stories, fables, poetry, intuition, foresight, hindsight, superstition and fact which makes up our Scottish heritage. Not surprisingly, over the years and in my travels across Scotland, I've had interesting encounters. There have been shy brown clad Picts seen in the gloaming, in amongst trees near Brechin.

I've spotted big blond Vikings stomping around the streets of Shetland; seen weary Roman soldiers, longing for home and for the sunshine and olive groves of Italy, sitting despondently by a ruined fort near Peebles; and I've encountered a brown-clad monk or two in the various abbeys I've visited.

I've seen other things, too. Once, I saw a whisper of bright fairies in, of all places the most likely, a garden centre. They danced amongst the bedding plants, cheekily swooping by the shoppers with their laden trollies. Amused, I saw a white-haired man brush one off his face, as if swatting an annoying fly, without looking up from the selection of watering cans he was examining.

I've seen a goblin sitting cross-legged in a park in East Lothian, his odd, pointed face bright with life beneath his floppy green hat. I've encountered some less pleasant sprites, bogles and imps dotted around in shop doorways, parks, near rivers, under arches, and next to dustbins. They know I see them, sometimes they touch me, or follow me for a while, but mostly they just look. I always smile, which seems the best way to deal with it.

I even have the occasional visit from a very grumpy guardian angel called Cynthia, who materialises, usually at the end of my bed, from time to time. She isn't very helpful and tends to dwell on the negatives, without giving me much encouragement.

"I just knew this was going to happen," she said one night, not long after Alan and I separated. "You are a disaster area, emotionally speaking," she added, resting her sandalled foot on the bed post. I noticed that her wings were moulting again, which meant I'd need to have a hoover round in the morning. She was nothing like the golden-haired, serenely smiling angels of fiction and painting. Cynthia had tousled brown hair, grubby robes and a harp with some strings missing, which was usually slung around her back at an uncomfortable angle.

Oblivious to my irritation, she continued: "The trouble with you, Mary, is that you act first and think second. I have my work cut out getting you out of trouble, you've no idea…" She broke off to pick up a biscuit from my bedside tray. "I don't like digestives," she said through a mouthful of crumbs. "Can't you get those nice ones with the squashy orange filling?" she asked.

I sighed. Cynthia turned up randomly, usually to tick me off about something. She flicked through the layers of my life, criticising, complaining and very occasionally making helpful suggestions.

"Why don't you get a job overseas for a while, till things settle down a bit?" she suggested one day. I was trying to fill in forms for house insurance and wasn't in the mood for career advice. "It would do you good to get out of Edinburgh, away somewhere different, get a new perspective on things," she said, idly flicking through my bookshelves and pulling out the occasional book. I noticed that, as usual, she didn't replace the book in the correct position.

"But I need to stay here, I have things to sort out," I told her, irritably. "You're supposed to give me good advice and keep me out of trouble, not think up daft ideas."
Cynthia had turned her attention to my sewing kit and the jar of spare buttons. "This is good advice, it would give you a fresh outlook," she countered, tipping a cascade of buttons through her fingers. "Ooh, what a lovely set of pearl buttons!" she exclaimed, scrabbling for a card of buttons at the bottom of the jar. "Can I have them, Mary? My robes need something sparkly and pretty on them!"

I swear that Cynthia had adult ADHD. She couldn't focus on any topic for more than a few minutes. "Yes, of course you can have the buttons," I told her. "I'll even sew them on for you, if you just stop nagging me about going away!"

The worst time for Cynthia to appear was at mealtimes. She'd materialise just as I was cooking dinner, and apart from the hygiene aspect of loose, tatty feathers fluttering perilously near the food, she kept interrupting, and moving things.

"You should think more about the future and not dwell on the past so much," she said, dipping a moistened finger in the sugar bowl. "Have you any olives today, those nice green ones stuffed with garlic, maybe? Who's coming for dinner tonight? Should you be putting so much thyme in the stew?"

I sighed inwardly. No point in antagonising an angel, however wayward she was. I answered politely.

"I think about the past because it affects my present life, and my future. There are some green olives stuffed with pimento in a jar in the cupboard behind you, if you'd like some. I have two friends from work, Jill and Kerry, coming for supper. And yes, this is just the right amount of thyme to use. I'm following my mother's recipe, and it will taste just fine."

Cynthia flounced a little. "Ok, no need to be so snippy! I'm only trying to help you."

I stirred in the tomato puree and watched out of the corner of my eye as she opened the cupboard and opened the jar of olives.

"Mmm, lovely!" she smiled, popping several olives into her mouth.

Harmony was easily restored. Give her her due, Cynthia wasn't one to sulk, or bear a grudge. She was just around a bit too much…

I came home from work another day to find her lying along the couch with the cat, watching the Jeremy Kyle show and tutting loudly at the guests and their life stories.

"These people make you look as if you've had a very dull life, Mary!" she commented, plumping up a cushion.

I went to put the kettle on. She liked Earl Grey tea of an afternoon.

As I waited for the kettle to boil, I thought, not for the first time, how ironic it was that I should be allocated a guardian angel when I went along with the David Hume school of thought as regards an afterlife…

I've also seen more than one unicorn. Like Steven, I spotted one on The Meadows one quiet Sunday morning in autumn, on my way early to visit a friend who lived in one of the sandstone tenement flats in Marchmont.

It was at the time Steven and I were living in the Old Town, in the flat up the 96 steps, and life was bleak and difficult. I was glad to be out in the fresh air. The grass was smeared with the thin coating of dew which lingers after a frosty night, and the air was fresh and clean, the sky washed with blue, dotted with clouds.

The unicorn was standing quite still, underneath an old sycamore tree, watching me. He was a large beast with a winter white coat and massive black hooves. His horn was golden, and his breath came in puffs in the cool morning air. I approached him carefully and he remained still and calm as I walked towards him. I met his gaze, locked onto those huge, beautiful brown eyes, drank in his presence.

He spoke. Of course he spoke, I expected nothing less. His voice was strange, powerful, and gravelly, like a blues singer from the deep south of America.

"You are unhappy, child. You have been wronged, you have suffered. You have suffered longer and deeper than most human beings are called upon to do. But you have my word that you will one day find peace of mind. No human can ask for a greater blessing than peace of mind, child. It is worth more than any riches, any power and any fame. And you will, one day, have all the love and affection which you lack, which you crave, and which will make you feel complete at last. You will be able to be free, and open, and live a normal life."

He paused, and pawed the ground. "Do not look for love, or peace. These things will happen to you without you searching for them. You have tasks ahead first, and you must be very strong. You are strong, much stronger than you know or believe."

With that, he pawed the ground again, then faded away. I was left staring at the tree.

After that, I caught fleeting glimpses of unicorns from time to time, though not so frequently again in Edinburgh, or so near to people. The sightings tended to be in woodland, on hills, or near rivers. And none ever spoke to me again, though I knew that they saw me.

Every time I walk along from Summerhall or up Middle Meadow Walk from Teviot Place, though, I notice the statues of the chained unicorns at the entrance to The Meadows. Chained, because they are so powerful, and such objects of fear.

The unicorns which I saw were mighty, magnificent and fearless, and chained only with flowers, garlanded around their manes. I was in awe of them and admired them, but I was never afraid of them.

I turned back from my thoughts to talk to Steven again, who was quietly sipping his drink.

"Does Julie know any of this?" I asked him.

Julie, his wife of ten years and mother of their two sons, was a paediatric nurse. A lovely woman, very practical, down to earth and extremely kind. We got along well.

"No, can't say that I've ever mentioned this," Steven answered, smiling.

Hmm. I could see why not.

"Of course, I sometimes have very vivid dreams, and because I talk in my sleep, she's occasionally asked me if I was worried about anything."

We aren't a very tactile family – a hug on meeting, that sort of thing – but this time, I laid my hand on his arm.

"Maybe we can fix this," I said, and outlined my plan.

He sat, thinking, for quite a while. Then he looked at me again, and ran his hand through his cropped, auburn hair. Incongruously, I suddenly remembered the red-gold, soft curls he had as a little boy, and my eyes misted over for a second. He mistook my emotion, and held my gaze with his big brown eyes. He'd got the eyes from his dad, and they went well with his colouring, I thought, inconsequentially. Not often I'd been in a situation to be looking at him face to face and with such intensity. It brought me up short to suddenly be aware what a handsome man he had turned into, and I hadn't really noticed. My poor children, what had I done to them, how much had I ignored their needs, as I struggled through my own bizarre problems?

"It's ok, mum, we'll get through this. Life must have been just hellish for you, with all that going on. Maybe this is now the time to lay it all to rest." Steven spoke quietly, sensibly.

He's turned into a fine person, despite what's happened, said the voice in my head. I usually knew who was talking in my head: often Aunt Jessie, occasionally others from the past. This time, though, it was my own voice.

We ordered some food, and another drink, and laid the plans, as best as we could. So much depended on help from Aunt Jessie, and we couldn't just email her, or send her a text. I had a suspicion that we wouldn't able to Skype with her, either...
When Steven and I finally parted that evening, I felt as if a weight had started to lift from my shoulders. It was still attached, but I could feel the lightening, the beginnings of optimism fluttering around, like a small flock of tiny chaffinches just out of reach, pretty, joyous in song.

I went by the herbalists and asked for a number of items. The chemist said: "Now, don't take any more than the stated dose, and don't take them both at the same time. Read the instructions very carefully, and be sure to drink plenty of water. Are you sure this is what you want?" I assured him that I'd be very careful.That night, I lay in bed, having taken both the draughts I'd bought earlier in the day and willed my mind to clear itself of any dross. I visualised the trivia of the day: shopping lists, laundry, Facebook, the novel I was reading, my forthcoming dental appointment and even my current plans regarding Brian Kelly, and pictured myself putting all of this in a giant black rubbish sack, and tying up the top.

I thought only of Aunt Jessie, her voice, how she looked, the things she said when I was a child, and what she said to me when I lived with Steven in the Old Town flat up 96 steps.

After a while I fell into a light doze, but was wakened abruptly by someone shaking my arm, quite roughly.

"You silly girl. The chemist told you quite clearly not to take both preparations at once. You will have a very sore head tomorrow!" Aunt Jessie looked cross. "You always were headstrong, Mary McGregor!"

I sat up in bed. She was right, I did feel quite dreadful. But it had worked, and Jessie was here.

"You told me many years ago that you'd help me when the time was right," I said. "This is the time, Aunt Jessie. I need to right the wrongs as best I can, so there can be peace. I'm weary. My son is haunted and troubled too, and he is blameless."

"Steven has a great gift," replied Aunt Jessie. "We will use it to the good, to rebalance the past."

She touched my arm: "You didn't do anything wrong about Jamie. It was just a terrible accident. I think that can be undone."

She paused, then looked at me, holding my gaze. "What you did by burning the letter meant for Elizabeth, though, that was wicked. It will take much more effort to put right, and you must be prepared for failure.

"It seems to me that you are using your own skills to clear your name of the killing of Jennifer Wilson. I don't need to help you much there, but I will do something to aid you on that matter, when the right time comes."

I began to speak, but Jessie raised her hand.

"It is a big effort for me coming forward like this to see you, and I can't stay long tonight. I will make contact with you soon and tell you what to do about the drowning of Jamie." She began to fade and shimmer around the edges, and in seconds, the room was empty, leaving just me and my throbbing head.

Three days later, I came home to find a letter, written in a fine ladylike hand on sepia parchment, lying on the kitchen table. Beside it was a waxed packet, sealed and tied.
The letter was from Aunt Jessie.

"Dear Mary," it read. "You must first deal with the accidental drowning of Jamie McGregor. After that, we will attempt to help your sister Elizabeth .You must do it for her, not yourself, and you need to keep your moral compass pointing due north. Your peace of mind is not as important as that of your poor sister, who lost the man she loved, and went to her grave believing he didn't care for her.

"Also, although your life has been blighted by Brian Kelly and the others, you must bear in mind that Jennifer Wilson died, which brought great and lasting sorrow to her family. This isn't all about you."

She never could resist giving me a ticking off, I thought wryly. I read the rest of the letter and the instructions very carefully, and examined the waxed packet she had left for me.

Next day, I went to the National Library and pored over old maps. I photocopied the ones I needed and added them to my folder. The day was bright, so after a trip to the main city library on George 1V Bridge to double check a few facts, I headed to my favourite spot in Greyfriars Kirkyard to eat a sandwich and think things over.

I first rubbed the nose of Greyfriars Bobby's statue for luck, as many thousands of tourists do each year, and then picked a spot in the churchyard to sit down. Being familiar with the terrain, and respectful of the dead, I didn't sit on a flat gravestone but on a small, fold-out waterproof sheet I always carried with me, placed on the grass.

The graveyard was quiet, it being out of tourist season, and I was mulling over my notes when Mary appeared. Once more, she hovered a little above the grass.

She seemed more agitated that usual, and when she spoke, for the first time, I could hear some sounds.

"You must help, you must help me," she said over and over.

I stood up and reached down to the child. I couldn't feel or touch her hand, it became misty as I stretched out my arm, but I felt a strange tingling and burning up through my fingers. "Mary, we will try, we will try tonight. Please give me all your strength tonight, please give Steven all of your energies and let your love for your brother Jamie burn strong and high and bright tonight." The child gasped, then smiled, for the first time in all our encounters, and left abruptly, no fading or gradual disappearance. After she had gone, I sat in the peace of the churchyard for some time, gathering my thoughts, clearing my head of irrelevancies. Steven told Julie he was meeting me for a drink again that night, as I needed some advice from him over my savings investments. She didn't question it, as she had no reason to ask for any more details. Like I say, Julie is a nice woman, who wished me well and had made no judgements.

We met this time near the Meadows, in a small pub, noisy with students. Steven ordered two glasses of orange juice and asked for glasses of tap water as well. Into the water, we quietly and unobtrusively tipped the contents of the two twists of paper Aunt Jessie had left me in the waxed packet, and set out into the Edinburgh evening.

We walked across the virtually deserted Meadows, hearing the occasional bird call and the distant sound of traffic.

The trees rustled high and black above us as we moved off the footpath and headed for the darker corners of the Meadows, as far away from the overlooking windows of the sandstone tenements as it was possible to be. I took out a small torch and the old maps, and using these, we walked still further. The sky was black velvet, studded with diamonds, and a faint wind blew through the winter night.

"This is the place. This is where the Borough Loch was, right here's where the pathways ran." I motioned to Steven to stop. We stood under an ancient sycamore tree, silent, and still, and waited.

For a few minutes, nothing happened, and I started to think this had all been a foolish, preposterous notion, a fantasy. Steven had been leaning slouched with his back against the gnarled bark, when he suddenly stood upright, alert.

"Look!" he whispered. "Look there!"
A faint, but increasing, light was coming from behind the trees, illuminating the grass where we stood. As we watched, a shimmer of water appeared, bounded by pathways and drainage canals.

The sun came up, showing the winter scene. The air was frosty, and I felt suddenly very chilled. A man was walking a dog, and two children, a girl and a small boy, were playing on the path. The boy had a stick, and was pretending to attack the older child.

It all happened so fast. The dog bounded away from his master and rushed onto the path, barking all the while. The little boy screamed and ran and then stood, rocking, poised on the edge of the pathway next to the murky, cold water. Then, his screaming stopped and he froze, his small body rigid with fear, his head tilting back at an odd angle. I was immobile. I wanted to run, to rush and save him, but my legs wouldn't work. My ankles felt as if someone was gripping them with an iron first. I simply couldn't move a muscle. I opened my mouth to shout but couldn't. I was the invisible, powerless, silent ghost here.

As I watched, paralysed, Steven flew across the grass and onto the path. With not a half-second to spare, my son scooped the child up into his arms just as the toddler lost his footing. The girl was screaming "Jamie! Jamie!" over and over, sobbing, as Steven set the howling child down safely on the grass. The dog walker had by this time tied up his animal to a tree and was by Mary's side.

"Oh lass, I'm so sorry," he said, "Is the bairn alright?"

The man turned to look at Steven. "Thank you sir," he said. I saw him look again at Steven, look at his clothes and shoes, but was too preoccupied to take in what he was actually seeing.

Mary stopped crying. I watched as she and Steven too looked at each other, for longer.

That night, after Steven had hailed a taxi home, and promised to take the next day off work, on some pretext, to allow him to rest up – he looked ghastly – I took a lurching red double decker back to my house. The normality of the journey home, with people yawning, clutching shopping bags, reading the evening paper or locked into their iPad worlds, drew me, shuddering and trembling inwardly, back to reality, back to the present.

I took no more pills or powders that night, but drank a pint of water before sinking into a mercifully dreamless sleep.

I texted Steven the next day, using guarded language.

He replied that he was fine, just resting up for the day as he felt very tired.

It was several weeks before I returned to Greyfriars Kirkyard. I'd been busy with my plans regarding how to deal with Brian Kelly, and also needed a mental and emotional interlude before tackling the problem of Morningside Mary and the letter.

However, the sun was shining one day so I took a stroll through the old churchyard, listening to the bird song and enjoying the peace.

I sat in my usual spot, face turned up towards the sunshine, eyes closed and mind drifting. I sensed Mary before I opened my eyes and saw her standing only feet from me. My eyes were blinded by the sunlight, which seemed to radiate and flicker around the child. She was smiling, and by the hand she had Jamie.

This was the ragged child who ran barefoot through the Edinburgh streets, in the gloaming. I am this child, she is me, I was her. I welcome her, for the first time, into my waiting arms, fold her back safe into that inner place inside my heart where she has somehow always lived. I hold the child close and safe, she puts her arms around me. Her child's breath is soft and sweet and her hair brushes my cheek.

Then, she pulls away gently, still holding my hand for a few final seconds, and she smiles, a beautiful smile.

Mary and Jamie lingered for a moment, then both waved their hands to me as they faded away, then disappeared entirely.

I sat, weeping, with joy, with relief, with gladness for a wrong righted, a sorrow averted, lives changed for the better. I sat for some time, thinking, wondering, until I heard the church door opening and a party of visitors emerging into the beautiful Edinburgh sunlight. Then, I gathered up my bag and drew out my mobile phone, to text Steven.

I only said four words.

"It worked. Thank you."

*****

Mary Ritchie put aside her knitting – a man's thick woollen jumper - and took her youngest child, James – called for his Uncle Jamie – onto her lap. She pushed her unruly hair back under her headscarf, and stirred the open fire with a long brass poker. Although she was now 30, Mary still looked like a young girl, her red hair undimmed and her eyes sparkling. "Well, ma bairn, would you like a story, one out of ma heid? Just before your sisters get in from school?"

James nodded and stuck his thumb in his mouth with great purpose. He liked his mother's stories almost as much as the toy horses and tiny swords and his dad made for him out of wood.

"Well," said Mary, cuddling her wee boy nearer, "here's a story about your family, before you were ever born, or your sisters, and before your da and I were married. When I was a wee girl, I lived with Granny and Grandad McGregor up in the High Street, with your uncles and aunties."

James listened intently, even although he had heard the story before. He sucked his thumb vigorously. "One day," his mother continued, "Granny McGregor asked me to tak' yir Uncle Jamie fir a walk. He wis jist a wee laddie, only a bit older that you are now. Ye'd nivir think it to see the height o' him now, or the strength he has liftin' and chiselling thae big stanes along wi' yir granddad McGregor, but Jamie was a tiny wee laddie, awfae small fir his age. Yir granny used tae aye be feeding him up. We walked awa' across tae The Meadows, ye ken where we go a picnic sometimes? In thae days, there wis still a lot o' water there, afore it was all drained away, and Uncle Jamie and me were having fun playing aroond on the grass and on the paths next to the water.

"Well, suddenly this muckle big dug came rushing along towards us. Jamie was awfy feared o' dugs in they days and he let oot sic' a skirl and a scream and rushed away frae the dug. Ah couldnae grab hud o'him! Jamie just suddenly froze, like a' the breath was oot o' him, and his wee pale face turnt blue. He did that sometimes when he got a big fright."

James's eyes grew wide and round. He knew what was coming next. Mary continued. "He was jist aboot tae topple into the water – and mind it was freezing cauld winter time, so if he hadnae drowned richt awa' he would hae got tangled up in the reeds growin' at the edge of the water and died o' the cauld afore we could get him oot – when suddenly this man came running like the wind oot o' the trees. Ah hadnae noticed him when we were playin' aboot, so he must hae jist got there.

"Anyway, this man scooped Jamie up in his airms and carried him ontae the grass. I wis crying and screaming, and Jamie had wet his breeks wi' the fleg he got, but he was alright. The man was wearing awfae funny claes, no' like ma da wore, or even like the claes the fine gentlemen wore that I used tae see goin' into the Sheriff Court up the High Street. He had awfae short hair tae, like ma brithers when they got the heid nits and had tae hae their heids shaved. But this man didnae look dirty.

"He gie'd me a look but didnae say anything. Funny, come to think, he had a look o' yer grandad McGregor aboot him. The same red hair, but something aboot his e'en an' a'."
James waited for the ending of the story.

His mother continued.

"Well, the man wi' the dug telt me to wait a minute, and he ran off tae his hoose, wi' the dug. Jist as weel, because Jamie wis starting tae greet again, just lookin' at the beast. The man came back in a minute or so wi' a blanket, and his ain laddie tae help, and he carried Jamie a' the way back tae oor house, wrapped up cosy in the blanket.
" Granny McGregor was in an awfy state when she saw Jamie, and me greetin' still, but we were both jist fine after a sit at the fire and some hot milk."

Mary paused.

"The man that saved your Uncle Jamie, he just disappeared as fast as he arrived. Ah wis cuddling Jamie while the man wi' the dug went off ta his hoose, and when I looked around tae thank the man with the strange claes, there wis nae sign o' him."

Mary resumed the tale, seeing her little son's eyes growing wide with anticipation.

"And who do ye think the man wi' the dug was? And who dae ye think his laddie was?"

"Ma granddad Ritchie and ma da!" shouted James, triumphantly.

Mary smiled at her little son, and wound one of his red gold curls round her finger.

"Aye, Mr Ritchie and his wife, yir granny Ritchie, got to be freends wi' Granny and Granddad McGregor, and I got to be freends wi' yir da. And when we grew up, yir da and me got married…"

"And then ye had Elspeth and Margaret and me!" James crowed in triumph.

Mary lifted her beloved son off her lap, and put the big black kettle over the fire to boil. The fire flickered in the cosy room, as Mary and James waited for the return of the rest of the family.

Chapter Seventeen *Saving the Letter*

Aunt Jessie had warned me this would be the most difficult task to complete, and that the outcome might not be as satisfactory as for High Street Mary. I had to try, though, I had no choice but to try to make this come right. I thought of all the misery which had followed on from Walter's death. My poor sister Elizabeth had grieved so long, and then hardened into herself. She had never married, never even had another sweetheart. She had stayed with Mother and Father until eventually they died, then she lived alone, turning eccentric and reclusive, a figure of fun amongst the local children, and a sad old lady to be pitied. Hers had been a blighted life, a wasted existence.

I just had to try to change history. Aunt Jessie was, fortunately for me, around a lot at the moment. It must have been very tiring for her, having to keep coming back over to this side to help out her favourite niece, but I was finding it increasingly easier to contact her. This would only work if I could get back to a point before Mary burned Walter's letter to Elizabeth. The timing was critical, and because I wasn't as gifted as Steven, it would be much more difficult for me to return to 1854 that it had been for him to go back to the eighteen century and save Jamie. This had to be my task, though, my son had done enough.

"Oh, tell me what to do, auntie!" I exclaimed out loud one night, as I tossed and turned through the midnight hours and into dawn. No word came back to me, though.

Nothing. Perhaps I had to do most of this by myself?

My stomach knotted as I got out of the car up in Morningside. I was too near to Brian Kelly's house and could sense the rising anxiety curdling my blood and bones. He was for another day, another time soon, but I had to focus and concentrate on Morningside Mary at the moment.

I walked by her old house. Nothing stirred, there were just blank windows looking silently over a neatly planted, terraced front garden, with old stone steps leading from an iron-railed gate up to a heavy wooden door. I was about to turn away when I heard the faint sounds of children, coming from the rear of the house. There was a high wooden gate set between the gable of the house and a stone wall, so I wasn't able to see into the back garden.

On impulse, I went up the steps to the front door and rang the bell.

A young woman in her thirties answered. Her long blonde hair was twisted loosely in a knot on her head and she wore paint-spattered jeans and a man's old flannel shirt.

"I'm so sorry to trouble you," I said, "but I'm doing some research into my family tree and have discovered that some of my Victorian ancestors lived in this very house. I wondered if I might briefly see round the house sometime it was convenient for you?"

I noted the woman's face registering surprise and slight wariness, before her expression cleared and she smiled broadly.

"Well, you've come at a good time, actually," she said. "The house is going up for sale next week and I'm just giving the garden furniture a freshen-up." She gestured down to her jeans and laughed. "The house is nice and tidy for once: the children have been warned it needs to stay this way for a while, too!" she smiled. "I'm going to have to get used to people going all over the house for the foreseeable future, so you are welcome to come in and have a look round just now."

"Well, only if you're sure…" I said, carefully wiping my clean shoes on the doormat. Politeness always pays off.

The woman said her name was Trudi, then asked a few questions about my ancestors. I told her as near to the truth as possible, without mentioning my previous lives.

"My great-grandfather lived here with his family in the second half of the 19ᵗʰ century," I explained, "and I'm just curious to see his home."

The woman led me through the hall, and into the sitting room. The intervening owners between John McGregor and the current occupant had retained many of the original features of the house, and I recognised the ceiling rose, the elaborate cornicing and the lovely old mantelpiece set above the open fire.

The current owner showed me round the house. The kitchen was modern and unrecognisable from the original, although the old window shutters remained. The other rooms were much as I remembered, apart from central heating radiators and other modern comforts. The house had kept all of its original fireplaces, though clearly they weren't in use, and even the bathroom had been sympathetically modernised with a Victorian-style roll top bath with claw feet. I was just walking up the last flight to stairs behind Trudi, to what had been my bedroom in 1854, when we heard sounds of screaming, coming from the back garden.

"Oh Lord!" said Trudi. "That's them fighting. Kids, eh? I'll need to go and sort it out. Please have a look round – this is the last room – and I'll put the kettle on once I've restored peace!"

She hurried back down the curved, narrow stairway and left me to go up the final few steps and into my old bedroom.

It seemed much smaller than I remembered. Of course it did! As with my previous, recent encounters, I had to keep reminding myself that I'd been a small child, and obviously, everything seemed smaller. The bedroom belonged to a girl, probably the one bawling her head off in the garden. I guessed she was around seven or eight years old, judging by the Disney duvet cover, the collection of dolls on, yes! the very same mantlepiece over the fireplace where I had arranged my dolls and other treasures. The fireplace was still there too, with its shiny dark green tiles and a small brass-railed fender. Sitting on the hearth and blocking the unused grate was a large doll's house. I suspected the girl was a little too old for it now, but reluctant to part with it. Some things don't change much. I was looking at the old cupboard door in the corner of the room in which I used to keep my toys, and wondering what the modern occupant kept in it – it seemed very nosy to look in – when I heard the faintest of sounds behind me, an almost inaudible rustling noise.

Before I even looked around, I knew it was her. It was Mary. She wore a plain navy cotton dress and a white pinafore, and her auburn hair was tied back with a matching dark blue velvet ribbon. She stared at me.

"I think I know you, but I'm not quite sure who you are... but why are you in my room?"

I smiled at her. She always was direct, feisty, and she wasn't frightened. I just loved her to bits.

No time to think this out, or to wonder how and why now, I just had to do.

I crouched down, so I was level with the child. I could see her trying to figure out what was going on, and almost getting there, but not quite.

"Mary," I said. "You must listen to me very carefully, and you must do what I say. I haven't time to explain everything to you, but you know how you remember living in Edinburgh before, down the High Street, and how you see things other people can't?"

Her eyes widened, but she kept on listening.

"Something will happen quite soon which will affect your family," I said. "You must do the right thing, Mary, or things won't work out properly in the future for you or the people that will follow you."

I looked at her hard.

"I know that you are angry with Elizabeth because of your punishment for snooping," I said, watching her gasp.

"Yes, you'll just have to believe me that I know what's going on," I said, smiling. Instinct told me I just had to keep going through this surreal experience.

"Walter will give you a letter for Elizabeth soon, just before he goes away to war. It is very, very important that you give your sister this letter. One day, you will understand why. I can't explain at the moment, but it is very important you stop being angry with her and make sure she gets the letter. Do you promise, Mary?"

She stared at me and nodded her head.

"Are you from the future?" she asked. "You wear very funny clothes and your hair is awfully short, for a lady!"

I smiled again.

"You'll understand all this soon enough, Mary. Now just promise me you'll give Elizabeth Walter's letter."

Mary smiled back.

"I promise", she said. "I do know you," she said. "I should be frightened, but I'm not. I don't know exactly who you are but I think you are telling me something important, so I'll do what you say. Would it be alright if I gave you a hug just now?"

I held out my arms to this dear child, who is also in me, who was me, who is me, who has sent me strength and intelligence and humour down through the genes, the DNA. I felt her small arms around my neck, and I held her close.

And then she was gone. The room was empty again, and I heard faint sounds, of laughter this time, coming from the garden. I slowly made my way down the twisty stair, then down the next set of wider stairs, and out into the garden where I had a cup of tea and a chat with Trudi, and watched Miranda and Simon squirt each other with water pistols.

I slept well that night, better than for a long time.
In the morning, I saw a note by my bed, from Aunt Jessie. Written as usual in her beautiful copperplate handwriting, on sepia paper, it said:
"My Dearest Mary, You have successfully accomplished this mission. You will discover how and why soon. I'm very proud of you, my dear. Hearts won't be so badly broken now.
"I know you have a final task to undertake, with the business gentleman from Morningside who wasn't always a gentleman, and still isn't a gentleman in his heart. I will help you a little with this when the time is right.
"With affection, Aunt Jessie."

It was several nights later when I woke in the night, pulled from sleep by sounds. Whoever thinks that ghosts, spirits and visitors from the other side are quiet needs to think again. Some do slip around silently, but others make a terrible racket.

It was Anne, a ghostly pharmacist who died in a car crash in the 1960s, who had visited me once or twice before, and who occasionally put thoughts into my head, usually in a fairly bossy manner. She seemed to have dispensed with the need to be discreet and delicate, because she banged my door shut behind her and landed with quite a thud on the end of my bed.

"Hi," she said. "I'll come straight to the point. Your auntie is a bit worn out with all this coming and going, dipping in and out of the past and future as she has been doing, writing you notes and suchlike."

I was about to speak but as usual, Anne just carried on, not brooking any interruptions. "Yes, I know she's your auntie. She kept it quiet for quite a while – bit of a dark horse, isn't she! However, she let me in on the whole story one day, she needed my help with a couple of things."

She shifted uncomfortably on my bed. "This mattress is very lumpy, time you got a new one!"

Furniture advice from a ghost. What next? Would she pop up next to me at IKEA to advise on soft furnishings, offer spirit guidance on supermarket shopping bargains or help me when I'm next buying a new pair of boots? I smiled to myself.

Oblivious, Anne continued.

"Jessie asked me to visit you. She's very proud of the way you managed in Morningside, and how you got Mary to come forward. Now, you need to see what happened afterwards, so you can close that chapter.

"You have to go to the old Royal Infirmary, you know, where they've converted the old hospital into flats and built all those apartments and penthouses. Go to The Meadows, just behind the building, tomorrow night about ten o'clock. It will be dark by then, and you've to position yourself in among the old trees."

She smiled.

"I know you still have the hardest task of all ahead, after this, but you must just keep faith. Good luck!"

And she was gone again.

The next day, I walked around the back of the old Royal Infirmary building, admiring the way Victorian and contemporary architecture had been blended to make a striking new mix of flats and shops. The sun was shining hazily, glinting off the windows of the new apartments. I passed the usual mixture of dog walkers, mothers with buggies and students lying on the grass as I strolled behind the building. I noted where I should be that evening, and went on home for a nap.

Waking several hours later from a dream inhabited by unicorns garlanded with flowers, being led down the Royal Mile by a group of bare-foot, ragged urchins who laughed and danced all the way down to Holyrood, and were welcomed into the Parliament building for juice and biscuits, I made coffee and dressed warmly for the night ahead.

The last rays of the setting sun were glazing the rooftops of the city's buildings, as I set out for The Meadows. A velvety dark sky soon emerged, soft and enveloping, dotted with stars. It was very like the night when I was here with Steven, when he rescued Jamie from death.

I chose a spot where I could lean against the rough bark of an ancient tree, and waited, listening to the night birds, and the distant noise of buses and cars making their way along Melville Drive. All was peaceful and quite serene. I lowered myself into a sitting position on the ground, cursing myself for not thinking to bring my usual fold-up mat to sit on. I closed my eyes and let my mind drift around, thinking of my children, and the Marys, and wondering how I could get Brian Kelly to tell the truth, on the record. Jessie said she would help, but I wasn't quite sure how even her skills would stretch that far. He wasn't a stupid man…

I began to be aware of a faint sound of voices near me, increasing in volume every second. Opening my eyes, I was surprised to see the inky blackness of the night had given way to a blue sky, strewn with small white clouds. I thought of Lilian, my tiny, long-dead sister from my time in the High Street, and how my mother said the baby was sitting on a wee white cloud above our tenement.

A light wind blew, rustling the leaves in the trees. I kept still and watched, as, like a pond's ripples subsiding, the scene before me clarified. Sitting under a nearby tree, on a spread-out rug, were several young women, all in old-fashioned nurses uniforms. They were having a picnic, and quite a lavish one at that. There were glass bottles with rubber stoppers, filled with what looked like ginger beer; sandwiches, apples and a large cake. The women, who looked to be in their early twenties, were laughing and chatting.

I sat very still, uncomfortably so, until I realised that, just as I'd been an unseen bystander before on The Meadows, when Steven saved Jamie, these girls couldn't see me. I was here only to observe.

"Well, thank goodness that's over!" said one girl. "This last lot of tests was so hard, but at least that'll be us through our probationer year, with a bit of luck!" She bit into an apple, with great relish.

"I'm glad we came over here from Infirmary Street to have the picnic," said another girl, leaning back against the tree, her eyes closed. "Gets us away from the smell of all that antiseptic and carbolic soap for an hour!"

"Now, Jean, you've got to admit that since Professor Lister insisted on all of these hygiene improvements, we've lost far fewer patients to the sepsis," said the girl sitting next to her.

"I love being back here," spoke a girl pouring out a glass of ginger beer. "London was tremendous, and I loved doing my training at the Florence Nightingale School of Nursing and Midwifery: that's such a mouthful, isn't it! I learned such a lot, but I'm so pleased to be back here in Edinburgh and working at the Royal!"

It was Mary. She looked so like Phoebe, the last time I saw her, that is, that flame coloured hair and sparkling eyes, the knowing smile, looking just as she had done at the age of seven. Mary had turned into a fine young woman.

I listened intently.

"Why did you go to London, Mary? Was it because of Florence Nightingale?" said Jean. "She did so much, didn't she?"

Mary paused, then began.

"Well, it's a strange story really. My older sister Elizabeth had a sweetheart called Walter, who died in the Crimean War. He was very badly wounded, too badly to survive, but we heard that he was tended so well by Florence Nightingale herself and her nurses in his last hours that I was inspired to take up nursing when I grew up. Luckily, my father felt that I deserved the chance to train at a worthwhile career and he supported me while I was in London."

She laughed. "My grandmamma in Troon almost had an apoplectic fit when she heard that I was going off to live in London and to train as a nurse! 'Not the thing at all for a young lady,' she had told mother and father. But my parents, especially my father who believes very firmly that women should be educated, felt it was a good thing for me to do."

"Oh, your poor sister," said Jean sadly. "How dreadful to lose her beau in that way."

"It was terrible," said Mary, "but she knew that he loved her. That was a funny thing too, the letter he left her before he went to the Crimea."Her voice tailed off for a moment, but the women around her sat quietly, waiting to hear the story. "I was very cross with my sister at that time, because she'd landed me in trouble with my mother and I was being punished," said Mary, "but just a day or so before Walter came to the house for what turned out to be the last time, I had a kind of dream, or a vision, I'm not sure what…"
"A ghost?" said Jean. "No, not exactly," said Mary. "It was a woman, she looked very like my Aunt Jessie, but a little younger and wearing very odd clothes, what looked like a man's suit, and her hair was short, almost like a boy. Anyway, in this dream, or day dream, whatever it was, she told me that Walter would give me a letter for Elizabeth and I must hand it over, or there would be difficulties for people in the future."
"My goodness, weren't you scared?" asked another nurse.
"No," said Mary, slowly. "I knew her, somehow."
Well dealt with, Mary, I thought, chuckling inwardly. If these girls only knew about the things you have seen, they would be flabbergasted.

Mary continued with her tale. "Anyway, a couple of days later, Walter came by the house briefly and left me a letter for Elizabeth, just before his regiment left for the Crimea. I did think about throwing the letter on the parlour fire to spite my sister, but remembering the strange lady's words in my daydream, I decided to hand over Walter's letter. Elizabeth cried a lot when she read it, but they were tears of happiness: he promised to ask for her hand in marriage as soon as he returned from war."

Mary paused again before resuming the tale.
"It was just ghastly when word came that he'd perished from wounds he suffered at the battle of Sebastopol. He had been awarded a gallantry medal posthumously for saving several of his wounded men by dragging them to safety. Apparently he had been terribly brave, showing immense courage on the battlefield. Although the doctors and nurses tried to save him, his wounds were too severe and he died in the field hospital. Elizabeth was inconsolable for many weeks and months, but eventually she began to recover gradually from her loss. Walter's fellow officer and best friend, Philip, visited her to talk about Walter, about his last hours in the military hospital, how much he had loved Elizabeth and so on."
"What happened to your sister?" asked Jean.

"Well," smiled Mary, "eventually she and Philip began courting and they were married five years ago. They have two little sons, and they called their first boy Walter. Fortunately, Philip has a permanent post at Edinburgh Castle now, and is unlikely to have to go overseas to fight again, we hope!"

"That's a very sad story," said one of the nurses, brushing cake crumbs off her uniform. "Dreadful about Walter, but your sister has a lovely husband and family now from the sounds of things. Just as well you didn't burn that letter, Mary!"

I saw Mary smile. "Now we are all grown up, Elizabeth and I get along together just fine, and I just adore my nephews!" The women sat, enjoying the sunshine and throwing crumbs for the birds, which came quite close to the picnic, and soon disposed of any remaining food.

"Well, I suppose we best go back to the hospital," said Jean with a sigh. "Just because we had these tests this morning, I don't suppose the Lady Superintendent will let us slack off this afternoon." The young women reluctantly rose from the grass, gathered their belongings, and still chatting, they moved away across The Meadows, slowly fading from my sight.

The breeze dropped, the sky darkened back to black, and I was alone once more, under a tree in The Meadows.

I was never to see Morningside Mary again, but I did learn one more thing of interest about her life.

Some months later, I was back at the city's main library, researching the history of medicine in Edinburgh in the 19th and early 20th centuries for an historical crime thriller I planned to write, when my eye was caught by her name. There was a photograph of her as well, in sepia, so I couldn't see her red hair, but I was sure it was her. The caption read: "Nursing Superintendent Mrs Mary Cameron (neé McGregor), the first woman to be appointed to the post soon after the Edinburgh Royal Infirmary moved to its new building in Lauriston Place. Mrs Cameron, who trained in London and Edinburgh, is married to Mr Albert Cameron, a consultant surgeon at the Royal Infirmary. Mr and Mrs Cameron have two sons, and live in Inverleith."

I smiled to myself.

Chapter Eighteen *Revealing the Truth about Brian Kelly*

I just couldn't see how to work this. Brian Kelly was critical to the revelations, but why should he confess to a long-ago crime which wasn't going to show him up in a good light, and might even lead to police interest? He had a reputation to maintain, a standing in the community, a respectable place in society, not to mention a wife and family.

I had been walking on Arthur's Seat, a chill wind whipping round my face, pondering, wondering, and letting my thoughts run free. Now, back home, I sat with my recorders and notebook, consolidating all the information I'd gathered and looking at it with a critical eye.

The evidence from Robert Scott and Beryl Wilson was fairly damming but it wasn't enough. Brian Kelly had to come clean for this to work. Aunt Jessie had been conspicuous by her absence since we'd resolved the Morningside Mary situation. Probably even spirts need to rest up now and then, and she'd certainly done a good deal for me recently. I went to bed and tried to switch off all trivial thoughts, and focus on Brian Kelly. I was due to see him again in a few days' time, taking with me a draft article and collecting old photos from him, taken during his early business life.

"Wake up, Mary," said a voice in my ear. Jessie was leaning over me. The bedside clock said three am. Oh well, ghosts keep their own times, I suppose.

She spoke quickly. "I said that I would help you when the time came for you to confront Brian Kelly. My original idea was to create a potion which you could slip into his drink, to make him speak the truth to you, but I think this is too risky. He is not a good man, Mary, despite his fine house and his nice clothes, and I'm afraid you might be at risk of harm from him. There is a darkness about him and I fear for your safety."

Jessie paused, then continued.

"I've made up a draught for you instead, Mary. There are risks for you with this, but it will give you heightened awareness and intuition and a very sharp brain for about three hours, then the power will wear off gradually, for an hour. You must be sure to be in a safe place, preferably your own bed, by the end of four hours, and you must rest up afterwards for a couple of days. I will leave you a bottle of medicine to take once you are safely home."

Crumbs, what has she cooked up this time? I wondered, but knew better than to question her ways.

Jessie patted my arm lightly, smiled and faded away.

Sure enough, in the morning, were two bottles by my bedside, carefully labelled 'before' and 'after'.

Brian Kelly once again opened the door of his villa to me, and ushered me back into the lounge. He offered me coffee, which I declined, being awash with Aunt Jessie's concoction, taken half an hour earlier. It tasted foul, reminding me of the cough syrup of my childhood, but with a hint of something else in it.

We chatted, and while he read my draft piece, I looked at his collection of old photographs, grainy black and white images of young men working on the backs of huge television sets, and of his first van, emblazoned with the name of his fledgling company.

I felt the draught working, a slow change at first, but gradually I felt my thoughts begin to race and clarify. I knew what to do. Once more, I reached into my jacket pocket and switched on the tiny hidden recording device.

"I need to talk to you about something else, besides your business," I said, in a cool tone. Brian looked up from my draft piece, looking surprised at my change of voice. "Yes?" he asked, a wariness evident.

"The death of Jennifer Wilson. It was you who flung the brick which killed her, not Mary McGregor. I want you to admit it," I said, switching on the larger cassette recorder which I'd placed on the coffee table.

 His face turned paper white, and for a moment or two, he was silent. Then, he seemed to gather himself, and I was reminded that he had been a street-wise toughie before he made his money and gained a veneer of respectability.
"I told you before, Mary McGregor did it, the wee girl from next door. It wasn't me."
"You liar," I said, coldly. "I'm Mary McGregor. You flung the brick at me, and Jennifer turned her head at the wrong moment and caught it on her temple. You lied in court, you and your family intimidated the other children, you blamed me and I was sent off to a remand home. I need you to admit to me that it was your fault."
He smirked.
"And what makes you think that I'm going to admit to that now, even if it was true? You are one crazy woman, Mary McGregor, if that's who you really are."
"Oh yes, I'm her alright," I said, feeling the anger stoking inside me, like a low fire being poked back into life.

"I need closure on this," I said. "My marriage ended because my daughter found out about my time in the remand home. I don't see her anymore, and it's because of you!"

He stared at me, the smirk still playing around his mouth. It was all I could do to stop myself from slapping his arrogant face, very hard.

Then the set of his face changed, and he lunged forward, grabbing the dictaphone from the table and expertly destroying it, in seconds. He paused, then grabbed at my jacket, wrenching out the hidden miniature recorder from my pocket. He flung it to the floor and jumped on it until it was cracked and crushed.

"Do you think I'm a complete fool?" he sneered, sitting back in his chair. I pretended to be upset, and crushed, and dabbed at my eyes with a hanky. Aunt Jessie's potion was working beautifully. "Oh well, I hoped you might tell the truth, just so I could tell my daughter and build the bridges with her, and see my granddaughter," I said sadly. I looked at him. "I can't prove anything unless you admit it, Brian," using his name for the first time. "It is so long ago, we were children, but it has changed my life," I said, looking down at the carpet, with every appearance of being cowed. A beautiful Axminster, I thought, inconsequentially. I raised my gaze again to meet his.

"I'm sorry, Brian. This was a stupid thing to have done. It was never my intention to go to the police, or any other authority. It was only for my family to know the truth."

He smirked again.

"You always were a stuck up wee madam," he said, "thinking you were smarter than us."

Oh, but I was. That's why you all hated me.

"Oh well," I said, making as if to gather my things together. "Secrets, eh? I suppose we all have them. Tell me though, when you flung the brick, did you mean to kill me?"

"No, of course not," he said. "It was an accident. I wanted to give you a right sore face though. But you'll never prove it was me. Your precious family can go on thinking their mother is a bad bitch."

"Well, I hope you can live with your conscience, Brian" I said, "knowing you've wrecked my life."

He smirked again, a horrible, condescending grin. The worst thing he could have done.

"When I boot you out of here in two minutes, I never want to see or hear from you again, young lady! Any more of this and I'm going to the police," he snarled.

Young lady. My skin shrivelled, his patronising, superior tone chilling me to my innards.

Slowly, I tore off a sheet of paper from my notebook.
"On this sheet, I want you to write following:
'I was responsible for the accidental killing of Jennifer Wilson in 1958. I aimed the brick at Mary McGregor with full intention of injuring her, but the blow struck Jennifer. I lied to the police and the court and I regret my actions. Signed Brian Kelly, dated 12th March 2018.'

"Now, why would I do that? We've had this conversation. Get the hell out of my house right now," he shouted.
Calmly, I laid the sheet of paper and a pen across at his side of the coffee table. I looked at him again, holding his gaze.
"Because if you don't write this confession, which I give you my word will only be used to clear my name with my family, I will feel obliged to tell Marie about Doreen and the affair you had with her," I said, icily. "Oh, and the abortion you made Doreen have. And you a good Catholic too! I don't suppose Marie's old dad will be too pleased to hear about it either. Wasn't it him who set you up in business in the first place? And I guess your parish priest, not to mention your pals at the golf club, won't be very chuffed either."

I had taken a huge gamble, based on guesswork, observation of Doreen's sad, single state, and some leaps of imagination. Fortunately, I'd landed spot on the mark.

Brian Kelly again changed colour, this time to a ghastly shade of grey. His mouth opened and closed like a goldfish, and it took a few seconds before he could speak.
"How, how did you know? That stupid cow Doreen…" he croaked.

"There you go again, Brian, blaming someone else," I said calmly. "You were a married man with two children, yet somehow Doreen is at fault? You got her pregnant!"
I continued, pressing home my advantage.
"Just for the avoidance of doubt, Doreen told me nothing about the affair or the abortion. I know about this through other ways," I added cryptically. The other ways were simply my own intuition and powers of deduction, but I wasn't going to admit that, of course. He sat for a few minutes, staring into space, and his colour began to return.
The businessman in him took over.
"How much do you want to shut your bloody mouth about this?" he asked.

I looked at him and saw the wee guttersnipe he'd been and still was, truth to tell, for all his money. "Brian, all I want is you to state, in black and white, that you killed Jennifer. I want no money from you. I only want my family to know the truth, before it is too late and one of us dies."

I held his gaze firmly.

"This will be shown to my immediate family, no-one else. Once they have read it, I will destroy the sheet: I'll tear it up and send you the shreddings, marked personal, to your place of work. Before destroying it, though, I will make one copy, which will go into an envelope with my will, which is held by my solicitor. There will be a note attached instructing it to be destroyed unopened on my death.

"What I know about Doreen and you will go with me to the grave. I've no wish to upset your family, but trust me, I will tell your wife if you don't co-operate."

"This is blackmail!" he shouted, jumping to his feet, raking a hand through his hair. He looked very angry and I was quaking inwardly. "Correct," I said, coldly. "Now, please just get on with this and write these few words." Reluctantly, he did so, checking the wording with me every so often. He handed me the sheet of paper and I tucked it into my bag.

"Goodbye," I said, putting on my jacket and heading for the door. I paused, hand on door handle, and looked back at him. "And Brian, don't even think about hiring a hitman, having someone tamper with my car or anything else of a threatening or dramatic nature. The note to my solicitor will include a sentence saying that the letter should be opened immediately should I die unexpectedly, in unusual circumstances or if any foul play is suspected. My lawyer is a smart cookie and you'll have the police at your door before you can say television set."

"Fuck, you thought all this through, didn't you!" He was clearly very angry and upset, but underneath that was the faintest, grudging hint of admiration. He wasn't used to being bested.

I left as quickly as possible and drove away from his house. A glance in my rear view mirror showed Brian standing in his doorway, hands on his hips, gazing at my retreating car.

Aunt Jessie was right about the after effects of the potion. I took her advice, and went straight to bed once I got home, and slept for twelve hours solid, a long, dreamless sleep.

Waking, I had the mother and father of all headaches and just made it to the bathroom where I was violently sick, several times.

I slept off and on for the next two days, getting up only to take doses of the 'after' medicine Jessie had left me, and to be sick again a few times.

On the third day, I had some toast and tea and a long, hot bubble bath, got dressed and put my sweat-soaked bedsheets into the washing machine.

By days four and five, I'd ventured outside and along to the corner shop for milk and bread; day six saw me back on social media and watching tv, and on the seventh day, I began repairing the damage done to my life, to my family.

Chapter Nineteen *Meeting Louise*

On the seventh day I met Louise.

The first time, the last time, the only time I'd seen her before was the glimpse from the window of my flat in Tollcross, just when Alan and I were setting up home together. I'd thought about her sometimes, of course, over the years. There had been so many other things to puzzle me, and to deal with, that the thoughts of the woman were put into a box in my head and the key firmly turned.

On the seventh day, I went to the city library, to use the photocopier.

True to my word, I made only one copy of Brian's confession, to be kept by my lawyer. I was glancing over the single sheet as I walked away from the photocopier, not watching where I was going.

"Oh, I'm so sorry!"

I knocked the woman's open handbag with my elbow, tipping it off the edge of the table, spilling the contents across the floor.

Down on my knees, picking up her purse, comb and retrieving scattered pens, I felt her arm on mine. The light touch burned, seared through me, my cells bumping and jostling, blood racing in the torrent through my veins.

"It's alright, easily done," said a quiet, smiling voice.

Our eyes met again, the forty years in between melting away. Once again, that powerful, lighting bolt, that huge surge melting through me.

Of course she knew me, as I had always known her. It seemed almost foolish to begin the conversation of strangers, when we were already embedded, linked, and at one. But we observed the niceties, had a coffee, and started the chat.

We began properly that day. Our journey together started, just as I'd been promised by the unicorn, by the voices in the night, and by the spirits of the city.

On the seventh day, it came to pass. The beginning of the end, and the beginning of the beginning.

Chapter Twenty *Family Matters*

Phoebe's younger daughter, Alice Mary, climbed onto my lap and proceeded to festoon my hair with the daisies and buttercups she'd just picked. At two, she looked just like her mother had done at that age, with red-gold wispy curls and big blue eyes. She had the same colouring as wee Jamie McGregor, as Morningside Mary, and as Steven. The red-haired gene is very tenacious, and extremely dominant.

"Look granny, your hair is just the same white colour as the daisy petals!" exclaimed Alice, her chubby arms reaching around my head to stick a few more daisies in my hair, at strategic points.

"Ha, mum, she's got you spot on there, you can't hide age!" Steven looked up laughing from the balsa wood airplane he was assembling for his younger son, Ross. The boy was hovering impatiently beside his father's deck chair, willing him to finish the task so he could run off and play with his older brother Andrew, who was already rushing around the garden with his airplane.

Just then, Phoebe came into the garden, carrying a pitcher of lemonade and tumblers on large tray. Flora, her four year old daughter, followed her mother, carrying a plate of newly-made cupcakes and a big bowl of crisps.

My family sat round me on the grass, as the sunlight dappled through the fresh green leaves of the apple trees. Julie and Steven called their boys across, and Cameron emerged from his greenhouse where he'd been tending to the new tomato plants. He flopped down on the ground, and raised his face to the sunshine.

"Wow, it's so hot!" he mumbled, his arm half across his face.

"We can cool you down, Uncle Cam," said Ross, thoughtfully picking up the garden hosepipe.

"Oh, no you don't, you monkey!" said Julie, two steps ahead of her sons, as always.

We all laughed, and I half-turned in my seat to exchange a smile with Louise. She grinned back, and stretched her hand across the short gap between our garden chairs. Her hand was warm and light, and she squeezed my fingers with a brief, gentle pressure. I felt the ridge of her nails, the beauty of her bones, and the pressure of her ring. She dropped my hand quite quickly – we weren't given much to public displays of affection – but not before we'd exchanged a look.

I'd known love before her, twice before. The first love affair had been true and kindly, with a gentle person, but we both knew that it was not intended to last. The other relationship had been unsuccessful, but the experience had strengthened me in unexpected ways.

These were necessary interludes and experiences before the time was right for me to meet Louise.

In the moment before we both turned back to look at the children, I saw that her eyes were shining and I knew that my expression mirrored hers. For the first time in three centuries, these days I felt at peace with the world, and with myself.

I had eventually told Louise the whole story, one night when we were having dinner at my flat. We'd been out for the day, away down to North Berwick and out on a boat trip to the Bass Rock. The thousands of gannets screeched and swooped over the spume-flecked waves, or perched on the massive rock, as they had done for centuries.

Morningside Mary and her family had visited this lovely seaside town each summer, staying in one of the seafront hotels, I remembered.

I smiled inwardly, thinking there can scarcely be a place in Scotland I haven't visited in the last 150-odd years, one time or another.

Afterwards, we walked along the beach, then had an ice-cream, wandering along the wind-blown sea-front in contented, affectionate silence, before catching the train back to Edinburgh.

Normal stuff. Ordinary, even, except for one event.

As we sat finishing the ice-creams and looking out to sea, Louise took three shells from her pocket and pressed them into my palm, one at a time.

"I – Love – You", she said, smiling.

Most times in life, as my old neighbour Effie once remarked to me, we have to settle for peace and contentment. True enough, we have these fleeting moments of happiness, watching birds, or seeing a sunset flush the sky, doing a jigsaw with a grandchild, or potting up seedlings in a greenhouse.

But the shells in my palm that day, that was different. I actually heard and felt my heart thudding in my chest, and a rush of joy swept through my bones, my body, watering my eyes.

Dizzy with love, I smiled at her, but then turned away, looking out to sea while I collected myself.

This is what I'd been promised, then. This is what Aunt Jessie, bossy Anne the pharmaceutical ghost, the unicorn on The Meadows had all told me would happen. They just hadn't said how, who or when.

Maybe it was the gift of the shells, or the second glass of red wine that evening. Perhaps it was simply the right time.

Just as I had done previously with Steven, when attempting to explain my past lives, I tried to be matter-of-fact and calm while telling Louise something which was very far removed from the usual life-histories which new partners share.

She didn't scream, or run away, or mock me. She listened intently, sometimes looking sad and sometimes smiling, particularly as I described my antics running around the streets of Edinburgh and getting into trouble with my mother.

"I like the sound of High Street Mary," she said. "Lots of spirit: "Well, I like to think she's still around in me," I laughed," although I don't do much climbing over railings into Queen Street gardens these days!"

I looked at Louise across the table, and she looked back at me, her gaze steady.

"I wasn't able to be at peace, to be comfortable in my own skin," I said. "There were so many things to hide. I was afraid much of the time, growing up in the 1950s, there was so much I didn't understand, and couldn't explain. Then there was the remand home experience and everything that followed afterwards, with ghastly inevitability."I drank some wine. "Poor Alan," I said, my voice a little unsteady. "I must have driven him mad. He knew he didn't really 'have' me, but couldn't understand why. He didn't really do anything wrong, and truth to tell, I can't really blame him going after Carole." I paused, then continued. "Until I was able to show my children the evidence, Brian's written confession, and let them hear the tapes I'd made with Robert Scott and Beryl Wilson, I couldn't really expect them to believe me. Steven listened to the tapes first, then he drove through to Glasgow to let Phoebe and Cameron hear them, and to show them Brian's statement. He gave Phoebe the letter I'd written to her, and I believe she cried and cried as if her heart would break."

I went on to tell Louise that I'd shared the Brian Kelly information with Alan and Carole, as I had with Phoebe, Steven and my elderly parents, now living in sheltered housing in Perthshire.

There were many tears, many conversations and many apologies when I revealed the story. My father, and Alan, both wanted to contact the police and the procurator fiscal, to have the case re-opened, but I was firm.

"I gave Brian Kelly my word that I only wanted to clear my name with my family," I said. "He has not behaved properly, but I will. Now that you've seen the confession, I'll keep my word to him and destroy it. The tapes will go too, I don't want any of this lingering around any longer."

I didn't tell my family about Brian's affair with Doreen, or her abortion. I didn't mention my previous lives either. I recognise that sometimes there can be too much information, so the secret of my earlier incarnations remains with Steven, and with Louise. In fact, I didn't shred Brian's confession paper. Instead, I burned it in the grate of the fireplace in my flat, shortly after visiting my parents and telling them the story. It seemed a better, more final thing to do than shredding the paper. I sent Brian a letter to his office, thanking him for seeing me but saying the information he had given me wouldn't fit with well with the feature I was writing, so I had disposed of the interview with him. He would just have to trust me on this one, that the evidence was destroyed. Once they had cooled, I scooped up the ashes into an envelope.

I took a trip across the city a few days later and scattered the ashes, surreptitiously, in the grounds of the hospital where Jennifer Wilson had died. I'm not religious, but as I flung the ashes up towards the windy sky, I sent a message up to Jennifer, saying that I was sorry she had died before she'd had time to really begin her life. I stood for several minutes, watching the grey ashes being swept up and away, till they became specks.

When I finished the story, Louise reached across the table and laid her hand over mind. It was soothing, and warm. She smiled at me.

"I'm glad you told me."

She looked at me with her calm gaze, and smiled again.

"It's all over now," she said.

Chapter Twenty One *Life in the Now*

Phoebe wanted me to sell up and move through to Glasgow, when it became obvious a couple of years ago that my arthritis wasn't going to get any better, and probably set to become much worse. I had two flights of stairs to reach my flat in Marchmont and it was beginning to become a problem.

"Please come through here, mum," she said on the 'phone one evening. "Cam and I will look out for a nice wee house or a ground floor flat for you nearby. It would be lovely to have you near, the girls would be thrilled to have granny handy!' She laughed, then said, more seriously: "We've so much time to make up, mum. All those years we didn't have. I'm so sorry…" her voice tailed off.

"Now, Phoebe, we've been over this so many times. It wasn't your fault, any more than it was mine. We are making up for lost time now, and I'll visit you lots. I just don't want to leave Edinburgh," I said, quite briskly. "All my friends are here, my interests and social life."
Not to mention all my past lives, I added inwardly.
"What about staying with Steven and Julie, then?" she asked.

Steven had offered to convert and extend the garage of their home in Cramond to create a granny flat for me. I politely turned down that offer too.

I could picture Phoebe's anxious face at the other end of the 'phone, perhaps chewing the ends of her hair as she did when she was a child.

"Don't worry about me, darling," I said. "Something will come up."

Something did.

I'd had a couple of books published over the years, but my most recent book, a medical crime thriller, did much better than I or the publisher expected. It actually made some real money, especially when Channel 4 decided to adapt it as a three part drama. Time to move.

I sold the flat in Marchmont very easily, to an investor paying cash who wanted the property as a buy-to-let, no doubt planning to rent it to a succession of students. I stayed with Steven and Julie for a short time, while I viewed many houses and ground floor flats in various parts of the city.

None was quite right, somehow.

I finally looked at an old, neglected cottage down a small cobbled street in Stockbridge. The house had lain empty for some time following the death of the owner and the subsequent protracted inheritance dispute. It had a long, narrow garden reaching to the banking of the Water of Leith. At the foot of the garden was a falling-down garden shed and a couple of old apple trees.

The owner had sectioned off a piece of the garden for vegetables, which had sprouted and shot, and there was a small patio area with broken paving stones and a rusted garden table and chairs.

Steven, who had come with me to view the house, was doubtful.

"Quite a lot of work to do, mum," he said quietly. The estate agent showing us round was checking his mobile phone, and was just out of earshot. "It's been empty a long time, it needs central heating, rewiring and a new bathroom. And that's just for starters: you might need a damp course, probably a new kitchen at some point too…"

"Let me have another look at the garden," I said, "You go out the front and check out what you can see of the roof and guttering."

I walked slowly back down the garden, listening to the birdsong and a faint hum of bees amongst the overgrown flowers. In the background, the stream sang, soothing and in tune.

The unicorn was standing underneath one of the apple trees, his paper white coat dappled with sunlight. It was, I was sure, the unicorn I'd first seen on The Meadows, but this time his mane was tangled with a looping wreath of wild flowers made of daisies, buttercups, red poppies and forget-me-nots.

These were his only chains, very easily broken. His golden horn glinted in the sunshine. He didn't speak this time, but he looked at me with his huge, wise eyes, and lightly pawed the ground with his enormous front hoof. I smiled at him, but went no nearer.

A moment later, he was gone, and I was left looking at the gnarled branches of the apple trees.

After a minute, I joined Steven again inside the house. He was investigating the staircase.
"Would you manage these stairs?" he asked.
"Of course I will," I smiled.

While he took some notes and talked to the estate agent, I wandered back into the sitting room. The recesses at either side of the fireplace would do ideally for shelving to house books, and a rag rug would fit nicely in front of the fireplace. I would buy it.

The unicorn had communicated his approval, but there were practicalities to consider and the surveyor was summoned. He was candid in his report, describing the large amount of work requiring done and hinting darkly at high costs. None of it mattered. I knew that this was going to be my home and that everything would be alright, in the end. Which, after many weeks of building works, plumbers, joiners and painters, it was.

***

Louise and I are sitting in my garden, drinking tea and listening to the tranquil sound of the Water of Leith nearby, gurgling its way down through the city and out into the Firth of Forth. A blackbird sings from a nearby tree, his song more sweet and perfect than the most wonderful symphony any human being could ever hope to create.

We are in the now. I will soon show her the Victorian silver photograph frame I found in an old antique shop, huddled down some worn stone steps in Stockbridge, a few days ago. In it, I will place the photograph I was able to find and copy recently from library archives. It shows a young Aunt Jessie, hair pulled sternly back into a bun, posing with her colleagues at the apothecary's shop. Behind them are shelves and drawers reaching to the ceiling, and on counter are bulbous bottles with coloured oils and preparations, each with a brass label hooked around the neck with a tiny chain. The print, enhanced by my friend Andy the photographer, will soon sit on my desk, a piece of furniture which was a real extravagance, and cost an eye-watering sum of money. It's a Victorian roll-top desk with compartments for envelopes, tiny drawers and larger drawers, and a section of green baize intended for the inkwells and sealing wax. I love every moment I sit at it. Later, I will prepare a meal, as we are expecting Alan and Carole for supper. It is high summer, and unexpectedly warm, so we'll eat outside. A chicken salad will be followed by fresh raspberries which Louise picked earlier from the canes at the foot of the garden. It will be a leisurely meal, and we will watch the cheese slowly soften on the board, in the evening's warmth. The bottles of red and white wine will empty as we chat late into the evening and watch the sunset flushing the sky pink, then flaring it red, before all light eventually leaves.

Alan and Carole still live in their ultra-modern glass and steel flat overlooking the Firth of Forth. Alan has retired from teaching chemistry to truculent teenagers and spends his days happily, visiting family and friends and indulging in his new hobbies of painting and hill-walking. He has aged well, and seems contented with Carole. They are suited as a married couple, and he and I work better as friends than we ever did as husband and wife.

We'll chat about the world, Scotland since the SNP surge, our family, Carole's job, and the holiday that Louise and I will soon take to France. Eventually, weariness will overcome us all, and I'll ring for a taxi to take our guests back to their shimmering glass home.

Louise and I will do a little desultory tidying up in the kitchen, before yawning our way up the little twisty stair to bed, knowing that tomorrow morning will come, bringing sunshine and a little rain in the afternoon, if the weather forecast is right.

Tomorrow, we will have coffee outside on the patio – newly re-laid and complete with an old wrought iron French bistro table and chairs. Then Louise will return to her own house, to see to her cat and go about her life, work at her tapestry or her paintings, until we meet up again in a few days' time. When she has gone, I will sit in the garden and doze over a book for a while, pick salad for a solitary meal, watch some television.

Louise and I are older, of course. We are in the latter part of our lives, with less time ahead than behind us, like an old-fashioned glass milk bottle with two thirds of the milk visibly gone. But one third is still a lot of time, a lot of happiness, love and companionship.

We laugh a lot together, cry a little sometimes, and have an easy, nurturing and contented relationship.

We don't plan ahead, except to book the occasional holiday or tickets for a film. There is no point, as we don't know what is ahead. We may live for another 20 weeks, or another 20 years. We don't know what is before us, no-one ever does. I only know what has happened in the past, not what is to come. We enjoy each minute, each hour, each day which comes along, thankful to be together for this remaining part of our lives.

I stand up and stretch, the arthritis catching me, making me wince, and out of the corner of my eye notice a small flurry of fairies, down near the rhubarb. Well, that's a surprise, not seen them for a quite a while, and not before in my own garden. Nice. I hope they like it here and decide to stay.

With one of those coincidences you might expect in a city the size of Edinburgh, particularly given the area where I'd chosen to end my days, I have George, Fiona, Timothy and Saffron as near neighbours. I met Fiona in the charity shop where she still does voluntary work and we struck up an acquaintance, leading to a friendship as we realised we lived only a couple of streets apart. George is a man resigned to the life he has chosen and must continue to lead. He sometimes comes around to help me with heavier garden chores, and we chat afterwards over a cup of tea or sometimes a glass of wine.

"There's nothing actually *wrong* with Fiona," he confided one day as we sat at the patio table one golden autumn afternoon, watching the blue smoke rising from the smouldering bonfire of garden rubbish we'd lit at the end of my garden.

"She's a kind woman, works hard to keep our home, is an excellent cook and a good mother. She takes an interest in my job, particularly if I have a change of secretary…" He paused, clearly remembering the time he fell off the straight and narrow with his secretary, she of the violet eyes, curvy figure and husky laugh.

Drawing himself back to the present, George pushed his spectacles back up his nose into the correct position and continued.

"It's just that, well, is this it? Life isn't very exciting. I go to work, pay the bills, and try to understand the ways of my children. I'll be retiring eventually, and then what?"

I didn't answer immediately, but poured him another cup of tea and passed him a digestive biscuit.

"I think, George, that you have to look on the positive side of your life," I said thoughtfully. "You and your family are healthy, productive people who contribute to society. Saffron and Timothy will soon be finishing their studies and forging their own lives, and you and Fiona will have more time to spend together. You can work on reconnecting, having a bit of fun together now you don't have to worry about your mortgage and school fees."

I paused, then continued. "Try and remember what it was that brought you together in the first place, all those years ago, what attracted you to Fiona in the first place. You have much to be thankful for, and this is your time to enjoy life, and do all those things you've been putting off. I would guess that Fiona feels much the same."

This was naughty of me, as Fiona had also confided in me and said much the same as her husband had just done. What he didn't need to know, of course, was that she'd come within a shirt button of having a fling with another volunteer at the charity shop, a younger man with dark curly hair, a gold earring and a *penchant* for writing and delivering performance poetry. Irresistible, but Fiona had resisted him, and was now feeling thwarted and cheated by her secret sacrifice.

"You should book a holiday, just for you and Fiona," I said to George. "I'll pop round now and then and make sure those kids of yours don't burn down the house, and that the cat is fed."
He smiled, still doubtful.
"Go for it, George!" I laughed. "Have champagne in bed, go dancing, have fun together! No camping, a nice hotel, good food, and plenty of time to relax!"

They booked a mini break in the Lake District, and next time George was round, to help me mend the shed roof, there was a distinct spring in his step. I even heard him whistling as he worked…

I see fewer and fewer people from the past these days, just the odd fleeting glimpse of High Street Mary who flits past me sometimes in the Royal Mile, and the very occasional visit from Aunt Jessie, always in the small hours of the morning. But I know she feels her work for me is over, and I'm very grateful.

I don't know where I'll be going when I finally pass away, but I do know that I won't need to return again in another century, another set of circumstances. I can live out the rest of this life of mine, knowing that I've reached resolution and peace.

That wisest of men, David Hume, apparently had a change of heart when nearing death, and thought there might be a God after all. We none of us know until we pass over. I keep an open mind, but expect that wherever I'm bound, the unicorn with the gravelly blues singer voice, and decked with a wreath of flowers, will be by my side when I come to make that final journey.

THE END

Printed in Great Britain
by Amazon